"Why did you even give a ball? Was it before you knew the contemptuous character I was? And will you pretend ignorance, take the easy way out, when people ask why I have left? How will you explain throwing me out of your house?"

He stared into her angry, working face, his own scarcely less white with fury. "You tormenting wildcat," he muttered, half under his breath.

His grip tightened insistently and before either of them was aware of what was happening, she was in his arms and he was kissing her ruthlessly, repeatedly. After the first shock of surprise, Joanna began to struggle furiously, only to find herself unable to move.

THE SAXON INHERITANCE

Lillian Cheatham

FAWCETT CREST • NEW YORK

A Fawcett Crest Book
Published by Ballantine Books
Copyright © 1980 by Lillian Cheatham

ISBN 0-449-21608-X

Manufactured in the United States of America

First Fawcett Coventry Edition: January 1981
First Ballantine Books Edition: August 1988

THE SAXON
INHERITANCE

CHAPTER I

JOANNA MARLBERN HUDDLED miserably
in her cloak and faced a biting northeast wind
that reddened the tip of her small, uptilted nose
and brought tears to her gray eyes. She was a
pretty girl, but at the moment she was not at
her best, with a frozen, pinched look sharpening
the outline of her heart-shaped face. The cold
made her wonder at her wisdom in remaining
on deck, but she rebelled against spending another hour in her dark, airless little stateroom
below, her home for the past—how many weeks?
She had lost count of the time, but it had been
too long. The dozen or so other passengers who
had been her companions during the long sea
voyage had long since disembarked, but she had
no intention of remaining below any longer, and
Georgie, afraid of being left behind, huddled
close to her skirts, shivering in the unaccus-
tomed cold.

She peered over the side of the ship, watching
the unloading going on below her on the dock.

In spite of the seeming disorder, the work was progressing without delay. The boxes and barrels that had been brought up from the hold of the ship were being stacked and left awaiting their departure by dray and cart. The shrill, staccato voices floating upwards struck harshly upon her ears, familiar with soft, hissing Indian accents. The sharp, pale faces were foreign to her. The truth was that Joanna was homesick. Already, she missed the dark faces, the women's liquid black eyes above their veils, all of the smells and sounds of India. This climate was appalling, and she felt as though she could not endure it if it got much colder; and added to her misery, there was the further desperate uncertainty of what she would do if Lord Arkwright forgot them, or the date of their arrival, or just neglected to send a carriage to the pier to meet them.

To the sailors working among the riggings, her bright face with its changing expressions and remarkably revealing eyes was a pleasure to watch, just as it had been throughout the voyage. Joanna did not think of herself as pretty; in fact, she had been encouraged not to think of herself at all, but in spite of a face unfashionably browned by the Indian sun with a sprinkling of freckles across the bridge of her nose, she was extremely pleasing to look at. Her eyes were her best feature, being gray and fringed with black lashes and finely-arched brows. She did not know how they changed with her every mood, from a darkness that was almost black to a silvery-gray, nor that her sensitive mouth was an equally fascinating barometer to her thoughts.

Just then, a slight disturbance attracted her attention. She turned eagerly, hoping to see a coachman or someone who might be Lord Arkwright's agent. This man stepping aboard the *Rose of Calcutta* was obviously a gentleman, with a London cut to his coat. He stood out, among the merchants who had been calling on the captain all morning, as a brightly plumaged parrot would among a flock of crows. Tall, handsome, with the lean, muscular figure of a natural athlete, he was dressed in a waistcoat that seemed to be molded to his broad shoulders; closely fitting breeches, and a pair of gleaming Hessian boots. He carried a rich, fur-lined cloak tossed over his shoulder as though he disdained the cold. He had stopped to watch a sailor climb the rigging, and the wind ruffled his thick, dark hair. To Joanna, the word 'Corinthian' meant nothing, but a knowledgeable Londoner would have applied it to this man. She did, however, think him the most handsome man she had ever seen, and when she remembered the swaggering young officers back home in India, they seemed like tin-pot soldiers when she compared them to this man's natural grace and presence.

He had stopped a sailor to ask directions, and she saw they were looking her way. Surely *he* could not be Lord Arkwright's agent? But, yes, he was walking slowly toward her, a puzzled expression on his face.

9

"Good day, madam. I am Arkwright. Where is the child?"

Joanna was struck dumb by the words. The last person she had expected was Lord Arkwright himself, and she fought down a sense of panic. Without speaking, she lifted her cloak to reveal Georgie, clinging like a small limpet to her skirts.

"Good God! Doesn't he have any warm clothing?"

She shook her head mutely, and he bent at once to lift the child into his arms and wrap him in the folds of his cloak. "Where is Mrs. Martingale? Who are you?"

"That is Mama," Georgie piped up, burrowing his cold nose into the man's neck.

His lordship started and looked at Joanna more closely. "Are *you* Mrs. Martingale?" he asked uncertainly.

Joanna cleared her throat. She was literally physically incapable of speech, stricken silent by his lordship's unexpected appearance. Obviously, he did not know Caroline Martingale by sight, but also, she did not fit the mental picture he had of her. Joanna could understand why. Caroline had been known far and wide as a beauty, and she, wan, pinched and bulkily wrapped in a shabby cloak, was as unlike her late employer as one woman could be unlike another. Apparently, Lord Arkwright did not intend to waste any more time on her. He was already unwrapping Georgie from the folds of his cloak.

"I have made a mistake," he said crisply. "I am looking for a Mrs. Martingale. Is this child her son or not?"

"Yes," Joanna muttered huskily. "That is Georgie Martingale." Right now, that was as far as she could go with this cool, frowning stranger. "Can we find some place where we can be private?" she pleaded.

His eyes hardened. "I see. You are that anxious, then, to conduct your business with me, Mrs. Martingale? You aren't going to faint?" he added swiftly, as she swayed alarmingly.

"No, I am just cold," she whispered.

"I suppose you are unused to this climate," he conceded irritably. "Come along, then. My carriage is waiting on the dock."

"My—my trunk. Our t-t-things..." she called, hurrying to keep up with his long stride.

"My man will see to them."

His lordship's carriage was very smart, black with highly polished trim. Joanna noted appreciatively the matching team of highbred grays that were attached to the carriage, a liveried coachman standing at their heads. As they approached, a footman, also in livery, leaped lightly to the ground to assist them. Lord Arkwright handed Georgie to him, then turned to Joanna. As he did so, his hand brushed the bandbox she was carrying.

"Ah-h!" He sounded pleased. "You have a piece of hand luggage. Give it to me. Starnes will take care of it."

"No, thank you. I would rather keep it with

me." Joanna clung to her bandbox but to her astonishment, Lord Arkwright continued to exert a strong pressure to pull it from her.

Finally, conceding her the victory with a frown, he released it reluctantly. "Very well! If you insist!"

Joanna was surprised by his obstinacy. Was he so arrogant that he disliked being crossed even in the smallest matters? Apparently, he was still displeased with her, for he allowed her to climb into the carriage without his assistance and slammed the door behind her with a vicious bang. From the window, her eyes followed him warily as he moved off a discreet distance and engaged the footman, Starnes, in a vigorous conversation. He seemed to be giving the man a series of instructions, and finally Starnes nodded and moved away, walking at a brisk pace in the direction of the dock where the *Rose of Calcutta* was being unloaded.

The hothouse warmth of the carriage was deliciously welcome after the cold outside, and Joanna leaned back against the red velvet squabs, her head spinning. Beside her, on the seat, was a fur rug, and she touched its supple folds wonderingly. She hardly needed it since the carriage was warmed by a charcoal brazier at her feet. Georgie settled down with a sigh, tired and drowsy after his long, cold wait on deck, and put his head in her lap.

Joanna found herself dreading the inevitable talk she must have with Lord Arkwright. Apprehensively, she reviewed what she knew about him. It was very little, considering that she would soon be placing Georgie's—and her own—future into his hands.

Of course, she admitted, she should have told him at once who she was. She had hesitated because of the letter that he had sent in answer to Colonel Barton's, informing him of the death of his kinsman, Major George Martingale in India. The colonel wrote him for assistance with the passage back to England for George's wife, child and the child's nursemaid. His lordship's answer had been scathing in the extreme.

Since George had apparently left his family in dire straits, his lordship wrote, his relatives felt a moral obligation to care for the child and the widow, but that was as far as it went. They had no intention of assuming responsibility for a nursemaid. In fact, he added, it might do Mrs. Martingale a great deal of good to have to care for her child during the voyage.

It had been a harsh, ruthless letter, notably lacking in sympathy for the widow, and Colonel Barton had been embarrassed as much as shocked when he told her about it. Oddly enough, Caroline had reacted with fear. How much her fear of going home had to do with what followed Joanna did not know. In the end, it had been Colonel Barton's decision, not Lord Arkwright's, that she accompany Georgie to England, but it had been the colonel's wife who had suggested that she leave things as they were when the captain of the *Rose of Calcutta* mistakenly assumed his passenger was Mrs. Martingale.

"It won't do any harm to allow everyone to believe you're Mrs. Martingale," she explained. "The passage was booked in her name, and who's to know the truth unless you tell? If they learn you're the nursemaid, they'll treat you as a servant, and you're as much a lady as Caroline Martingale, any day."

The colonel, who usually made it a point of policy not to differ with his wife, agreed that Joanna would be wise to allow everyone to assume she was Mrs. Martingale. He also made the practical suggestion that she encourage Georgie to call her Mama. The voyage had hardly gotten under way before Joanna saw that they had given her good advice. The social pecking order aboard ship was rigidly enforced, and a pretty young widow with a child and noble kin in the background was respectable; a pretty nursemaid without a mistress to protect her would have been at the mercy of snubs and insults.

Her thoughts were interrupted as the door opened violently and his lordship flung himself into the carriage opposite her. His set, angry face did not invite confidences; in fact, he looked like a man who would be furious to learn that he had been deceived. Her confession died upon her lips. They were in Portsmouth, miles from London, and she would not put it past him to abandon her here and now if he chose to do so. Her mind shied away from the alternative.

In the light of day, her explanation now seemed unbelievably awkward. It had all seemed so simple to the Bartons, but what would this man think of her taking Caroline's place? Would he consider it a rashly impertinent act and refuse to employ her? Remembering his hard, bitter letter, his contemptuous dismissal of the nursemaid in his calculations, she thought he might. He was not a kindly man, nor a charitable one when he had been deceived. She sensed that instinctively.

By this time, he had shrugged free of his cloak and was stretched out in one corner with his long legs resting on the seat beside her. It was a discourteous position, and she suspected that he had assumed it deliberately in order to underline how he felt about her.

"Where are we going, my lord?" she asked carefully.

He looked out at the gray landscape, his scowl deepening. At first, she did not think he intended to answer her, then, "Mockridge Hall, for a start. After that, it depends upon you."

"Mockridge Hall?" How could it depend upon her?

"My estate in Surrey. How did George die?" he added abruptly.

"Of cholera, my lord. There was an epidemic."

"Indeed? How did it happen that you and the child survived?"

"He—er—George did not die at home. He was stationed at an outpost near the border for six months. Everyone at the outpost died."

15

"Indeed?" he drawled. "And what happened to his things?"

"His—*things*?"

"Yes! His gear! Clothes! Belongings! Surely you know what happened to them, madam?" he asked impatiently. "Were they burned?"

"Oh. No, my lord, they were returned home. At least, his clothing and bedding were burned, but his personal belongings, such as his boots, belts, saddle—that sort of thing—were all returned home. What a strange question!" she added wonderingly.

"But a justifiable one, surely?" he asked smoothly. "You are apparently destitute—without funds—so why shouldn't I ask if George left anything of value, anything you might wish to sell . . . now," he added significantly.

"Oh, I see." A hot tide of red covered her face. She did not see, except that Lord Arkwright was obviously a miser. He was wealthy, yet he was not above quibbling over a widow's few shillings. Why, altogether, George's bits and pieces would not pay the price of one of those thoroughbred horses pulling this carriage. A trace of ice tinged her voice. "I don't think there was anything left, my lord."

"Not surprising, remembering George," he murmured cynically. He seemed immune to her contempt, but was looking at her again, analytically, as though seeing her for the first time. "Amazing, that blush. It *seems* quite genuine. Can you summon it at will, or is it necessary to feel a slight degree of embarrassment first?"

"Not embarrassment, my lord," she replied coolly. "Whatever I feel now, it is not embarrassment, I assure you! Distaste, perhaps."

He gave a sharp bark of laughter. "Claws, eh? Fools write a lot of nonsense about India," he added disconcertingly.

"I beg your pardon?"

"Fools write a lot of nonsense about India," he repeated slowly, as though he was speaking to a child. "For instance, I have read that it has a very unhealthy climate, and that the sun's rays are extremely damaging to the skin."

Joanna raised enquiring eyebrows. "Yes?"

"And to a woman's complexion. Fools! You don't look a day over twenty."

Joanna flinched. His guess was amazingly on target. "My lord," she said hurriedly, "I—I must tell you. That is, I have been guilty—I have practiced a deceit—on the ship and when I met you. Because of Georgie, only, I assure you. He is such a baby, and I love him so much and—and—m-my lord, he has been my responsibility since he was placed in my arms within minutes after his birth. If I am at fault...and I admit that I may be...I assure you it is because of Georgie...."

His lip curled as he interrupted her torturous explanation. "Naturally," he remarked sarcastically. "I expected you to hide behind the child's shadow when you explained your—er—misdeeds. But perhaps I can anticipate your confession, since you are having such difficulty with it. In fact, I can almost write it myself! You are the best little mother in the world and cannot bear to give your child over to the care of cruel, heartless strangers, yet you can't afford to keep him with you because you have been left penniless. Am I right, so far?"

Joanna wondered if he intended to be deliberately insulting. "Yes. More or less."

"More, rather than less," he agreed mockingly. "Therefore, you must throw yourself upon the generosity of relatives to provide an allowance in order to keep your child. But naturally, the allowance must be commensurate with your position as George's widow and the mother of his son. His—er—heir. That position, of course, is an unique one, because of his relation to an elevated noble family."

Joanna was silent. So. It was intentional.

"It must cover the expenses of a life you believe is your privilege. Jewels, clothes, servants, luxuries! All of it! Am I right, so far, madam?"

Joanna bit her lips. "Not luxury," she said levelly, "and not for me. For Georgie. And why not? Doesn't he deserve your consideration? He is only a child. He cannot fend for himself. Is he, therefore, to be turned into the street? I cannot give him anything. I have no money. Do you not feel an obligation to provide for a child of your own blood when you have so much? Are you so—so miserly, that you can ignore an orphan, whose father gave his life in defense of his country?"

He laughed shortly. "I wondered when we'd

bring George's heroism into the conversation! Are you now trying to claim he was a patriot? Surely not! You forget, madam, that you are talking to one who knew George well, and of all persons, he was not cast in an heroic mold! Far from it! So, don't wave the flag at me or talk of obligations to a soldier's son! In fact, I would prefer to dispense with the sugary little platitudes altogether," he added roughly. "Be honest for once in your cheating little life. I can deal with a woman who is frankly greedy, but one who cloaks her greed with hypocrisy sickens me! As for the child, surely you don't intend to raise him to think of his father as a *hero?*"

Well, really! Platitudes, hypocrisy, greed—what a thoroughly cynical man Lord Arkwright was, to be sure! Joanna saw red. "Would you have me tell him he was a *coward?*" she demanded hotly. "George did die of cholera, my lord, I assure you! He was not executed before a firing squad!"

He shrugged, apparently unmoved by her defense. "Suit yourself. He is, after all, not my child. But don't try to act the solicitous mother at this stage! Colonel Barton left me in no doubt about your so-called maternal feelings!" Joanna bit her lips. "Your son was reared by a serving scullion simply because you were too lazy and indifferent to see to his welfare yourself. The good colonel more or less assured me that you would not be happy to take on his care aboard ship." He added contemptuously, "... which was precisely the reason that I was determined you should. Who was the creature whom you wanted to bring with you, anyway? One of George's cast-off wenches?"

Joanna gasped with sheer outrage, but Lord Arkwright added sardonically, "No, don't stab me with those eyes, madam! I know what sort of man George Martingale was, and too many people have told me about his conduct in India to have any doubt that you could have long remained in ignorance, either. In fact... but enough of this. I told you I did not care for hypocrisy! You were certainly frank enough about your demands in your letter."

"M-m-my l-letter?"

"Yes. I presume you received my reply?"

"Y-y-your reply?"

He frowned slightly. "Didn't you receive it? I assumed that was why you had the colonel write me instead of the duke."

Duke? What duke? By this time, Joanna was thoroughly confused, but wisely remained silent.

"I presume that you are disappointed because you did not get the reply you expected." Lord Arkwright had taken her silence for guilt. "I expect you wish for me to act as your go-between to speak to the duke?"

"T-t-the d-duke?"

"Are you in the habit of stammering?" he asked impatiently. "The Duke of Somerton, of course. He will not be so charitable about the child, so I advise you to lay your cards upon the table. He owes you nothing but what he chooses to freely give. The boy may be his heir, but your threats will not move him, and so I warn you, madam! Furthermore, if you are hoping to be taken into his home as George once was, you may forget it. He's never forgiven George for stealing from Somerlea."

Joanna gulped, dazedly contemplating what she had just heard. She had thought she knew the Martingale family inside out—Caroline, particularly, had never been secretive about her quarrels, her lovers, her debts—but neither she nor George had ever hinted that Georgie was the heir to a dukedom! It had not been like Caroline to keep her—or in this case, Georgie's—light under a bushel, either. Why, why? Was it possible that she had been afraid as Lord Arkwright had inferred?

And Lord Arkwright? Did he stand in line, after Georgie, as the duke's heir? Could that be the reason for his dislike? It would explain so much. How could she leave Georgie in the care of such a man?

"And you, my lord?" she asked stiffly. "What about your—obligation to George's son? Do you feel none?"

"I can't say that I do," he remarked dryly, "since I am not related to him. The obligation on my part is due solely to the Duke of Somerton, my cousin. Apparently, you do not know, but I am related to his grace because our mothers were sisters. George was a nephew of the late Duke of Somerton, his grace's father. We were both his wards, and both of us lived at

Somerlea because we were orphans. Time after time, my uncle had to rescue George from a scrape of some sort, and my aunt had to endure his tale-bearing and attempts to make trouble between herself and her husband. When the duke died of congestive fever, her position was made intolerable by George, who was the presumptive heir. Three months later, my cousin Miles was born, George was out, and my aunt made it clear he was no longer welcome at Somerlea. And before he departed England for good, George repaid all their kindness by stealing Somerlea's most treasured possession. I can assure you, neither of their graces have any intention of putting up with the same sort of thing from George's wife and son. Is that clear?"

"Perfectly clear, my lord." Her lips were stiff. "It is rather sad, however, for a five-year-old child to be burdened by so much hate."

Lord Arkwright frowned. "I have nothing against an innocent child," he said defensively. "However, he is not our concern. You are his mother. After we finish negotiating our business, you may be on your way."

Joanna's grip tightened protectively on the sleeping child. "Negotiate?" she asked unsteadily.

"Yes. We appreciate your negotiable position. You have something to—er—sell, in a manner of speaking, and we to buy. My cousin Miles does not want it to be said that he has failed in his duty to his heir. If you cooperate, he is prepared to make you a small allowance that will keep you both in comfort until the boy is of age. Along with that, he is prepared to deed over to you the title to a small cottage in the country near Stratford. Also, he will see to the boy's education when he comes of age. His only request is that you hand over the family heirlooms that have been left in your keeping, and thereafter keep yourself and the boy out of his presence. He is adamant that he must have your promise about that. If you wish, you may marry again, go to London, do whatever you like, so long as you do not use the name of Martingale, or allow your son to be identified as a Martingale. If your conduct becomes notorious in Stratford or in London, he will cut off your allowance and take your child away from you, leaving you to make your way alone. Is that clear?" he added curtly.

Joanna was stunned. She hardly heeded the reference to heirlooms—in fact, the word passed over her head since she knew nothing about any—but the coldly impersonal disposal of Georgie like so much unwanted baggage had shocked her. She longed to slap that handsome, arrogant face, to be granted the luxury of throwing his words back into his teeth, but she knew that for Georgie's sake she could not afford to lose her temper. Thank God, she vowed, that she had remained silent until she learned what sort of people would assume his guardianship. Well, she had learned, and obviously, between this man and his cousin, there wasn't so much as a pennyworth of difference. So much for cold, cruel charity!

Joanna looked out of the window as though for inspiration. Her hands clenched and unclenched on the ties of her bandbox as her brain seethed with words, words she longed to say, but somehow, instinctively, knew would bounce off this man's stony facade with all the force of a ball bouncing off a granite wall. No, she must be clever, and turn his insults back on him, hit him where it hurt, in his pride. When she finally looked up, her face was calm, and a half smile curled her lips, belied by her white face and glittering eyes.

"Apparently, since I am going to be forced to deal with you rather than his grace, I had better be quite frank, just as you have requested me to do." Her voice was sugary sweet. "First of all, I have no intention of being spirited away to a country cottage. I have been away from England too long to be satisfied with ruralizing. I long for gaiety, excitement, pretty clothes and the company of gay friends. I can get that in London, not Stratford, so I intend to live in London. I am glad to know that his grace will be generous, since it is possible that his idea of an allowance and mine might differ. Frankly, I do not intend to economize until after I have had my fling." Her laughter was an icy tinkle, although she was secretly appalled by the look on his face.

"Georgie and I must do a great deal of shopping. I am sure that a man of the world such

24

as yourself, conversant with women's fashions, can see that living in India as I have I have become sadly out of style. And, of course, apart from our clothes, I will need a house, servants, a carriage, horses, and perhaps even a few jewels. Merely enough to be presentable when I go into Society. And I see no reason to hide, nor to change my name, although I promise you I will be discreet, if possible," she added provocatively. "But I do want all of George's old friends to know that I am in town. You will be glad to know, however, that unlike George, I do not gamble, so the duke will not be put to *that* expense. Ah, let me see," she added hastily, as she caught a glimpse of his murderous expression, "that should cover everything, I believe."

"You have far-flung plans, indeed, madam," he snarled, menacingly. "May I be so bold as to ask what you intend to use for money?"

"Money?"

"Yes. Money. The duke has no intention of financing a riotous fling such as you envision, and you obviously have no money of your own. I can only presume that you have merchandise which you consider highly saleable?"

Joanna's jaw dropped. She had lived for years with a wanton—Caroline Martingale—whose favors had been bought with money and jewels while her husband had tacitly approved by looking the other way. To Joanna's innocent ears, therefore, his lordship's sneering taunt conveyed only one meaning, particularly in view of his earlier strictures about her conduct. Her face flamed and her eyes flashed sparks of fury. With an effort she controlled her temper and forced herself to reply coolly, "That is the least of my worries, my lord. I do not need to—er—resort to any extremity. Have you forgotten that my son is the heir of the Duke of Somerton, and whether the Duke likes the idea or not, I should not have any trouble getting credit." She remembered half-forgotten tales overheard from George and some of his fellow officers. "I can rent a house on credit, buy clothes on credit, and hire servants on credit. With my expectations, I can even purchase jewelry on credit!"

"And have you forgotten my threat to have your son taken away from you, madam?" he commented suavely. "Where will your precious credit be then if you no longer have the custody of the heir?"

"I am the widow of an officer who lost his life overseas in the service of His Majesty!" Joanna blazed in reply, forgetting for the moment that she was no such thing. "Does the Duke of Somerton really wish to create a scandal? Think of it. A soldier's widow, deprived of her child! Reduced to living in penury. I understand some scandal sheets will pay a great deal of money for that sort of thing. People like to read stories like that about aristocrats," she added, gazing limpidly at him. Elvira Barton would have recognized her mannerisms as being copied directly from Caroline Martingale, but Elvira's honest soul would have quailed to hear Joanna Marlbern talking like that. Joanna, however,

26

exulted at getting her own back when she saw the look of white-hot rage on Lord Arkwright's face. "Think what the gazettes could do with a story like that about the heir to the great Duke of Somerton! His mother starving in a garret, begging in the street!"

"I fear you are laboring under a misapprehension, Mrs. Martingale," Lord Arkwright grated between clenched teeth. "The duke is a young man, and will be soon marrying and begetting a child of his own. Your credit, and your sensational story, won't last any longer than the announcement of his betrothal! You will then be expected to pay your own way and the scandal sheets won't be interested."

"But I will have had my fling," she cooed. "And if I am not financed by the duke, then I will be forced to the—er—sale of that merchandise you mentioned," she added outrageously, drawn on to reckless lengths by the glitter in his eyes.

His lids drooped. "Now, there, I fear you have overreached yourself, madam," he drawled. "The duke is indifferent to *that* threat now that I have your luggage."

She shrugged. "What are a few dresses? I intend to buy a new wardrobe."

"But your household goods?" he asked significantly. "They are also in my possession."

"Do you imagine that I care?" She laughed. "No, I shall insist upon new carpets and bedspreads and curtains in my London house. And new china and—and linen, too!"

He flushed. "You are mighty cool about it, madam. Do you think I am bluffing?"

"Bluffing, Lord Arkwright? No. But do you think that I am? I assure you I am not," she added loftily. "I intend to see you squirm, you and that precious cousin of yours! Georgie has as much right to the name of Martingale as the duke does, and that is one condition I shall *not* obey, merely to satisfy that man's overweening consequence!"

"Indeed? George must have been an accomplished lover to provoke such loyalty from his widow," he murmured dryly.

She flushed. "We'll leave George out of this," she said crisply, "and concentrate on his son."

"Are you then, as arrogant on the subject of family pride as he was? Useless, when I hold *all* the cards," he added smoothly, leaning forward and lifting the bandbox out of her lap before she realized his intention.

"Give that back to me!" She bounced up indignantly.

"I think not." He was tearing it open as he spoke. He plunged his hand into the mass of paper, then his jaw dropped. His face was ludicrous as he drew out a bonnet, a simple little straw thing adorned by a bunch of red cherries and bearing a distinctly home-made appearance. "It's—it's a bonnet!"

"What did you think it was, you clumsy, wicked man?" Joanna's hand was trembling as she tried vainly to straighten the crumpled cherries.

"Certainly not a bonnet." For the first time, he sounded disconcerted and slightly ashamed. Tentatively, he tried to smooth the cherries and when he could not, tossed the bonnet impatiently into her lap. "Oh, take it! I have no wish to harm your silly bonnet, although it is just like a woman to mourn a crushed bonnet after she has been talking blackmail."

She scrubbed her eyes childishly. "If it's blackmail to demand justice for Georgie, then so be it. I can't support him, so why shouldn't his cousin help me? What—what if he was an orphan? His grace would be forced to help him, then, wouldn't he?"

"Oh, certainly," his lordship drawled. "Under those circumstances, his grace would probably send him as far away as possible to one of his outlying estates that he seldom visits, and put him in the care of a tutor until he can be sent away to school."

Joanna flinched. "Then Georgie is fortunate that he has a mother to fight for him," she said slowly, "since the sight of him is so offensive to the mighty Duke of Somerton."

"You think that justifies your threat to make a scandal?"

"I don't see why his grace should not share with Georgie," she countered evasively. "He has so much; we have so little!"

"Precisely the sentiment I would expect from George's widow." His lordship was ironical. "That was his philosophy. If I might be permitted to give you a word of advice, madam, I suggest that you close with our original offer. I do not intend to hold it open much longer, and I must inform you that by now your household goods will have been taken apart."

"And I have already told you I do not care!" She glared at him. A pounding headache was beginning behind her eyes, and his continued references to a few boxes of cheap bric-a-brac was irritating. "Altogether, they wouldn't bring more than a few shillings, so if you have had them torn apart merely to satisfy your grudge against me, then you are welcome to that satisfaction. After all, you paid to have them shipped, not I. There is nothing in them that I value."

"I—see." He sounded ice cold with rage, a rage that seemed inordinate under the circumstances. "I seem to have underestimated you, Mrs. Martingale. Obviously, you have made your preparations well in advance, or—they were made for you. Was this clever plan George's? Made in case of his death? I presume that you *will* let us know when you are prepared to negotiate?" he added ominously.

She merely shrugged wearily.

"It looks as though we are temporarily at a stalemate until we arrive at Mockridge Hall, when you can deal directly with my cousin."

"Is your cousin there, then?" Joanna asked uncertainly.

"But of course. He had not intended meeting you, but.... However, in case you are considering pleading for better terms, be warned. I am his adviser, and I have no intention of allowing you to bleed him dry to satisfy your greed. If necessary, I'll have you put in prison first."

With that, his lordship called for a halt and removed himself from the carriage, apparently preferring to sit outside with the coachman. By now, Joanna's headache had become a throbbing reality, and she attempted to relieve it by putting her head against the cushions and sleeping. It was impossible. That man's words, his last devastating threat, kept intruding themselves upon her thoughts. Altogether, she fumed, he was the most odious, hateful, arrogant person she had ever met, and his wickedness left George Martingale smelling like a rose by comparison!

CHAPTER II

THIRTY MINUTES LATER, Joanna was still angry although common sense had begun to assert itself as she realized the predicament she was in. Through her own indiscretion, she had thrown away her only chance to settle hers and Georgie's future. Earlier, her situation had been precarious, but now, she had a child to support—something she had not had when she began her journey today. Having no previous knowledge of the Duke of Somerton, she had drawn her own conclusions from what his cousin had said: young, arrogant and so blindly prejudiced that he hated an innocent child. To Joanna, that was the hardest of all things to understand, for Georgie was an extremely lovable little boy. He might wear his father's image stamped on his face but for Joanna, who had no reason to like George Martingale, that was immaterial. He was a child, and therefore, innocent.

She had always congratulated herself that

she could keep her temper, even under extreme provocation. Frequently, she had experienced harshness, for one could not live in a position of servitude under Caroline Martingale and not often feel the lash of her tongue, but she had never before lost her temper so thoroughly. But, of course, she reminded herself, she had never been accused of promiscuity, greed and hypocrisy, and although the words had been intended for Caroline, they had been altogether too personal for her not to react to their sting. She could have cleared up Lord Arkwright's misunderstanding about herself (although that would have left the problem of Georgie still unsolved), but she vowed that nothing, absolutely *nothing* would make her confess her deception if it meant throwing herself upon that man's mercy.

Others before him had made the same assumption as he did about her. A pretty girl in Joanna's position, serving employers who were notorious for their loose morals, was inevitably a victim to rumors about her own behavior. More than once, she had had to repulse unwelcome advances and listen to dishonorable propositions. She had grown adept at recognizing and rebuffing the men who made them. They had usually salved their pride afterwards by telling themselves that she was George Martingale's mistress, although, as a matter of fact, George had always behaved in a scrupulously correct manner toward her. He knew, of course, that if he forced her to leave, his son would have no one, and when his death and Caroline's disappearance left her without a protector, Colonel Barton had known that he must send her home as soon as possible to avoid future trouble.

Joanna had been fourteen when her parents died in one of the plagues that swept India periodically, and their deaths had left her an orphan. She had been cared for temporarily in the home of her father's commanding officer while an agent of the East India Company searched for the child's relatives back in England. He found no one. The child's paternal grandparents were dead, and he had no real clue to her mother's people, since Joanna could tell them nothing except that her mother had been Scottish. Her future had been bleak indeed when Caroline Martingale offered to take her into her home and train her as a nursery maid for the expected Martingale child. The solution had been hailed with relief by everyone concerned.

When Georgie was born, Joanna was given full charge of him. She had already learned that Caroline disliked the whole process of having a child and that it would be a kindness to keep the baby out of her sight. And now, for the first time, Joanna was given the answer to why she had borne the baby at all: his value lay simply in his position as heir to the Duke of Somerton.

Joanna reluctantly admitted that Lord Arkwright might have some justification for what he had said about Caroline and George Martingale. Despite her youth, she had never been blind to Caroline's and George's characters. He was a crafty manipulator and she was a wanton, and, apparently, rumors had reached Lord Arkwright. But, as she deliberately closed her mind to probable rumors and remembered instead his insulting, vitriolic contempt, his—his disgusting words about herself, she told herself firmly that *nothing* could justify such abuse. Courtesy demanded that he accord the widow at least an *appearance* of solicitude, no matter how he really felt.

She did not know his lordship well enough to know that he was thoroughly in agreement with her sentiments. Sharing a windy perch outside with the coachman, he was remembering his lack of restraint and was appalled. If she was puzzled by the degree of his dislike, he was even more so. As he huddled in his cloak and scowled at the gray landscape, he wondered how he could have lost his temper when he fully intended to remain in control. It could only be that woman, who had from the first seemed so unlike his mental picture of her. That had changed rapidly, of course, as her demands became more brazen!

Thanks to Georgie, who presumably knew his own mother, no flicker of doubt crossed his mind about her identity; he merely felt a moment of disquiet that he may have been given a wrong picture of her. He had to admit that her appearance had surprised him, for at first she had seemed more like a frightened child than an experienced heartbreaker. Which was surprising, since George had been somewhat of a connoisseur of women. His taste had run to a bolder type than this girl—woman—who had a rare, delicate prettiness, a sort of waif-like appeal. His lordship frowned slightly. Five years ago, he could swear, she would have been a child, scrawny as a rail, all eyes and elbows. How old was she, anyway? His eyes narrowed. Could that be the secret? Could she have been some base-born chit whom George had raped and then been forced by public opinion to marry when she was discovered pregnant? Perhaps, if he delved deeper, he might find that the marriage had not even occurred until *after* the baby's birth, when George learned that he had the son he craved. For a moment, he toyed with the thought of doing just that and confronting her with it, but he dismissed the idea as unworthy. *He* was not a blackmailer, no matter what the woman might be.

Anyway, he told himself firmly, if she had been innocent before George, she was now an accomplished cheat and a doxy who was an able foil for George's chicanery. Given time, she would seek her own level; find someone of George's ilk to take his place; perhaps even marry her, and thereby relieve his cousin Miles of his responsibility. However, and here his lordship's scowl grew even blacker, he must admit that in this first round of theirs, the chit had succeeded in scoring a point or two. Which meant exactly nothing, he reminded himself harshly, since he would inevitably win the battle.

Shortly after noon, a halt was called. They had stopped at a rustic country inn. Joanna, who was very hungry, awakened Georgie at once.

The door jerked open. "You'll stay where you are!" Lord Arkwright informed her shortly. "This is a primitive place—there's no private dining room."

"But I'm hungry," she began.

"We'll be in Mockridge Hall soon." The door slammed on her indignant face.

Georgie fell back asleep; but Joanna's stomach rumbled noisily. She was faint with hunger and her feelings weren't improved to see his lordship stroll out of the inn, a tankard of ale in his hand, wearing the appearance of a man well pleased with himself. He drained it hastily as a man rode up and hailed him. By craning her neck, Joanna could see that the man was Starnes and his well-lathered horse looked as though it had been ridden hard. He was no longer dressed in livery, but was wearing leather breeches and coat. Leaning forward with one arm on the pommel, he engaged his master in conversation which was abruptly terminated with a short, pithy phrase by Lord Arkwright. He strode toward the carriage, an expression of cold fury on his face, and Joanna drew back instinctively, absurdly sure that he was going to yank her bodily out of the carriage.

He did nothing of the sort, of course, and a minute later, the carriage started up with a jerk that almost flung her on the floor. The horses left the innyard at a fast gallop which continued for almost an hour. By that time, they had arrived at a small, quaintly charming village that huddled close to the walled grounds of a large estate. The road led past the estate for a mile or two, then turned in between a pair of handsome iron gates, surmounted by crouching unicorns. Mockridge Hall.

A woman and a child came out of the gatehouse and fluttered their handkerchiefs at the carriage, and the gatekeeper pulled his forelock as it went by. The road led through an avenue of trees, surrounded on either side by a wood. Joanna caught a glimpse of a startled fawn before the carriage pulled up, with a flourish, before the entrance of a Queen Anne manor house.

Joanna caught her breath at its beauty: two-storied, mellowed brick, with mullioned windows, softened by creeping tendrils of ivy, and glowing like a gem in its setting of trees and formal gardens. Two or three sheep were cropping the grass by the river which was shadowed by willows and several magnificent oaks with branches that trailed in the water. Today, the water did not reflect the trees: its surface was slate-gray and opaque, hardly distinguishable from the dismal sky above. But nothing, thought Joanna, could detract from the beauty of this scene: the clean, simple lines of the house and the wide, gracious sweep of the lawn. She opened her mouth spontaneously to say so as Lord Arkwright assisted her out of the carriage, but the sight of that stern face killed the words on her lips. He obviously had no intention of extending a friendly hand, and she could not either. He strode forward without speaking, leaving her and Georgie to follow alone.

Inside, he unbent a little. While Joanna divested herself of her cloak for the waiting butler, he knelt and disengaged Georgie's clutching fingers from her skirts. In a gentle voice, he suggested to the child that he go with the nursemaid who was waiting to take him to the nursery.

"Come with me, Master Georgie," the girl held out her hand. "Your supper be waitin' for 'ee."

Georgie left Joanna and timidly took her hand. Joanna watched him go in a tired haze. Apparently, Lord Arkwright's household was singularly adapted to deal with any demands made upon it, or as a more likely solution, he had small children of his own. Shrugging faintly, she turned away to find him regarding her with an oddly disconcerted look.

He was feeling peculiar, too. Divested of that awful cloak, Mrs. Martingale was even less like the beautiful woman he had been led to expect nor did anything about her ring true. Her face bore lines of strain which he supposed was natural enough, under the circumstances, but it did not make her look like a coquette. Her thick brown hair was inexpertly bound in a massive bun on top of her head and her white neck rose, childishly thin, from the collar of a particularly unattractive garment. Made of mud-colored stuff, it covered her from head to toe in a series of wide, thick flounces that added a foot to the width of the garment and made it as shapeless as a sack. Hardly the costume of a professional beauty, he thought, making a manful effort to control the spasm of emotion quivering in the corner of his mouth. No, Mrs. Martingale was playing a little game with them. By masquerading as a poor little waif in seedy clothes and cracked boots, she was attempting to gain their sympathy. It was most effective, he admitted analytically.

Joanna watched suspiciously the play of emotions across his face, ranging from puzzled amusement to finally, his habitual cynicism. She knew that the garment she was wearing was unfashionable, since Elvira Barton had found it in the bottom of a missionary barrel, but it was warm and it would have never occurred to her to wear it for an effect. At the moment, she was too tired to analyze what his expression might mean, however.

"I am ready for those negotiations you spoke of," she said wearily.

Lord Arkwright surveyed her coolly. Right now, she looked too tired to put up a defense. At the moment, she was ready to fall on her feet.

"I think not. Our negotiations will have to wait until I confer with my cousin. Meantime, you may be glad to rest. My housekeeper, Mrs. Blackwell, will show you to your room."

Mrs. Blackwell was an elderly woman clad

41

in a black silk uniform and wearing an air of respectability that would have reassured Elvira Barton herself. As they mounted the stairs, Joanna concentrated desperately on her small, erect figure in an effort to avoid stumbling from weariness. At the door to the bedroom, Mrs. Blackwell turned and regarded her approvingly. Apparently, she saw nothing wrong with the missionary dress.

"You'll want hot water and a tea tray. Go in and rest and I'll send someone up right away with both."

With a confused notion that she must not break bread in the house of her enemy, Joanna refused the tray but agreed to the hot water.

"What shall I do?" she asked desperately. "Does his lordship wish for me to come downstairs after I have washed? Will you ask him?"

Mrs. Blackwell looked shocked. "Oh, no, madam. His lordship will send for you when and if he wants to see you. In the meantime, you must rest in your room until dinner. I will send a maid to you to help you dress in time."

Alone at last, Joanna gazed around the bedroom with rounded eyes. She had gained a confused impression of grandeur downstairs but this bedroom, designed to pander to feminine taste, was the most beautiful she had ever seen. A soft shade of rosy pink dominated the color scheme with accents of gold. The chaise lounge was covered with downy cushions and the dressing table was littered with an array of crystal perfume decanters as well as a silver-backed comb and brush set. The windows, swathed in rose satin, looked out upon a balcony that in turn overhung a formal rose garden. A cold wind blew through the stark brown bushes, rustling the stalks and bending them almost double, but inside a glowing fire in the brass grate heated the room with a sensuous warmth.

She was a trifle surprised by the luxurious bedroom assigned to her, for considering Lord Arkwright's anger she would have expected a room under the eaves. She was too inexperienced to recognize that his lordship's revenge would take a more subtle form; that his pride would not allow him to treat her as anything but a guest so long as she was in his home. She did see, however, the impossibility of winning a battle with the owner of this magnificence, and sheer tiredness made her fling herself upon the bed and burst into tears.

A discreet knock brought her scrambling to her feet, searching for handkerchief. When the door opened, a smartly uniformed maid-servant entered bearing a covered tray and a can of hot water. Behind her was a lady, who made a place at the table for the tray and then, when they were alone, turned questioningly to Joanna.

Although of middle age, the lady was quite beautiful and bore a striking resemblance to Lord Arkwright. Her gown of amber crepe was in what Caroline used to call 'the first stare of fashion.' The stylish arrangement of the suspiciously jet black curls made Joanna's eyes widen, and they grew rounder as they traveled the length of the gown. It had a deep décolletage, a pleated bodice and a pencil slim skirt. The sleeves were long with tiny puffs at the shoulders and ended in deep pleated ruffles at the wrists.

"Do you mean that *you* are Georgie's wife?" she asked musingly. "Are you sure that you are Mrs. Martingale? I cannot believe it!" Then, as though the absurdity of her words struck her, she laughed. "But of course you are! But—you are not at all what I expected, although Simon warned me! How do you do, my dear?" She held out her hand and Joanna, warmed by the friendly words, took it hesitantly.

"How do you do, my lady?" For good measure, she added a curtsey.

"My lady?" quizzically. "Why do you call me that? I am Celia, the Dowager Duchess of Somerton, and Lord Arkwright's aunt, not his mother. No doubt you noticed the resemblance?"

Joanna twisted her hands nervously and nodded.

"And what is your name? I cannot continue to call you Mrs. Martingale, not a child like you!"

"I am Joanna, your grace." Joanna made another curtsey.

Her grace surveyed her covertly, her eyes mirroring her frank astonishment. Joanna's hair was escaping from its bun, her face was tear-stained and the mud-colored garment she wore was more like a nun's habit than the dress of a seductress. Yet, she had just been told by her nephew that this girl was a heartless, grasping little wench who was also promiscuous and calculating. Her grace made a lightning decision. Simon had made a mistake. It was quite possible, she thought tolerantly, for in spite of his experience with women, he was nevertheless capable of the most extraordinary misjudgments. This was one of them.

"I heard that you refused a tray," she said smoothly. "So I ordered one for you. You must eat. We dine early, but it will still be at least eight before dinner."

"Will I be here then?" Joanna asked bluntly.

Her grace's brows rose. "Dear me, Simon must have been crude indeed if you think he would countenance sending a guest on the way in such weather as this."

Joanna glanced at the window. A cold, stinging rain was flaying the panes.

"Now sit down, my dear. You must eat while the food is hot. It will make everything seem so much brighter, I assure you, after you've eaten something and had a good nap." She motioned Joanna to a chair.

"Does Lady Arkwright know that I am here?" Joanna sat down slowly.

"There is no Lady Arkwright. My sister Molly died when Simon was an infant and he is not married."

"That may account for it, then," Joanna murmured, cautiously taking a mouthful of the fluffy omelet.

45

"Account for what?"

"His smug—certainty that he is never wrong," Joanna replied evenly.

"Simon *is* dogmatic," her grace sounded amused. "It comes from having been indulged by my husband when he was a child, and then expected to take on the burden of surrogate father to my son while he was still a boy. It made him slightly pontifical at an early age. However, although I might doubt his wisdom in certain areas of speculation, I would have never questioned his judgment of women until now but—you are not the hardened adventuress he takes you for, are you?"

For a moment, Joanna was strongly tempted to unburden herself to this sympathetic lady. The words trembled on her lips but something held her back, a reluctance to yield the last barrier in her defense of Georgie.

"I would hardly admit to being an adventuress, would I?" she asked smilingly as she busied herself with pouring from the silver teapot.

"How old are you? I didn't know that Georgie's sins included robbing the cradle."

Joanna busily sugared her tea and added cream while she pondered how to answer. The duchess scented a mystery about her, and she must find a way to parry her questions without rousing her curiosity further. Her grace noticed the girl's evasiveness, and like Simon suspected that she had been a child-bride, but of even more absorbing interest than the issue of age was the riddle of Joanna herself. She was either an accomplished actress or a total innocent. Moreover, she had never remembered seeing Simon in the temper he had been in this afternoon when he stormed into the salon after seeing Mrs. Martingale upstairs.

"We have a ticklish problem on our hands, Miles," he had begun almost at once. "It's not going to be as easy as we thought with this Martingale woman. Starnes reported he found no sign of the Saxon Collection in her things—and he turned her trunk as well as the barrels of household goods upside down—and she refused to meet your terms. Instead, she made some outrageous ones of her own!" he gritted between clenched teeth.

The other occupant of the room, the Duke of Somerton, sighed and turned away from the window, where he had been gloomily watching the rain squalls. He was a young man of twenty who so closely resembled his cousin Lord Arkwright that he might have been taken for a younger brother. However, there the likeness ended, for his grace had none of the gallant manners or excellent clothes sense that distinguished his more worldly cousin. Like his father before him, he was a countryman, with a countryman's love for his land. He admired with something close to worship his cousin's skill in boxing and his judgment of good horseflesh, but the thought of further emulating Simon by attending an assembly or playing the pretty at a ball filled him with alarm.

"Did you gain any idea as to where she might have hidden the Collection?" he asked.

"Absolutely none! Oh, she is very clever! It is certainly not on her, so she must be sending it by someone else. A partner. George is dead and a woman like her wouldn't waste much time in finding a man to take his place."

"A—a partner?" Miles was dismayed.

"She must have one!" Simon asserted. "For one thing, she was insultingly confident that I wouldn't find it, and for another, she threatened to market the merchandise elsewhere if we didn't meet her terms! Which seems to indicate that she has the Collection safely hidden where she can get at it—or her partner can."

The duke drew a deep breath, a slight paling of the boyish cheek showing his emotion. "I can't let that happen," he said grimly, and for a moment, he looked older and careworn. "We'll have to meet her demands whatever they are."

His lordship swore violently. "It goes against the grain to give in to a brazen little strumpet like that, but of course, you are right. We are going to have to play her game until we have our hands on the Collection and then—Heaven help her! I'll see that little bitch in gaol if it's the last thing I do," he promised himself savagely.

Here, her grace took a hand in the conversation. "It seems to me that we must put our heads together and out-think her. Tell me again, what did Lieutenant Northcote say about her?"

"That she was a conscienceless hussy who was capable of anything; that she neglected her child; sold her favors to George's fellow officers. George kept a gambling hall in his home and it was her task to lure the younger fools there, and George looked the other way when she took one of them to her bed. So long as she made it worth his while, he didn't seem to care. Barry Northcote said that one of his friends, a Lieutenant Dalton, could not take it when she threw him aside for another officer who had more to offer. He returned to his barracks and blew his brains out. It made quite a scandal, and his colonel sent George to that outpost where he died. The woman was put on notice to confine her misbehavior to—er—one man in the future."

Her grace shuddered. "She must be an *awful* woman!"

An odd look crossed his lordship's face. "A— subtle one, I think. Oh, I can see how she was so successful with her alluring ways, for one would not guess she was a grasping woman. Frankly, her letter was so crude that I now think her confederate must have written it in her name. She would never have done it. I think she would surprise you, Aunt Celia, if you ever met her."

"But I am going to meet her. In fact, I wouldn't miss the opportunity for the world." His aunt rose and shook out her skirts. "I will go right up now."

"Aunt Celia, I don't want you to have anything to do with that woman. She can dine alone in her room after Miles and I have talked to her, then be on her way."

"I assure you, Simon, I am not a wilting violet." She was amused. "Neither do I need your protection. She may be vulgar and grasping, but I am quite capable of holding my own with her. And another woman may understand her nature where a man would not. Is she presentable?"

Her nephew made a slight grimace. "She could be," he said dryly.

His aunt now knew what he meant and began to understand the bafflement she had sensed in Simon when he spoke of her. Personally, she did not think any woman would choose to look this dowdy if she could help it, and that Joanna had meant there was more here than met the eye. She began to have a lively curiosity to learn what Joanna had said to Simon; what her mysterious 'terms' were.

Since Joanna was obviously exhausted, her grace rose and prepared to leave. "We shall expect you for dinner," she said firmly. "We dress informally, so an afternoon dress will do. Your trunk is downstairs and will soon be brought up. I presume you—have something—er—suitable?"

Joanna flushed. She had already realized that her stuff dress, one that Elvira Barton found in the bottom of a missionary barrel and deemed eminently practical for her trip was hopeless. "Most of my things are unsuitable for this climate," she said stiffly, "but I have a muslin dress."

"A muslin dress will do fine," the duchess assured her. "I will send my maid in to help you dress and she will bring you one of my shawls to wear over it."

After she had left, Joanna prepared to take a nap on the luxuriously soft bed. But she could not sleep. Too much had happened to her in a short time. The voyage, and before that, the elopement, and then, the terrible news of Caroline's death.

It had been hot that morning, the morning when the colonel and his lady called to tell her about Caroline. The sun was filtering through the slatted blinds, heating the bamboo furniture with bars of light and shadow. The flimsy curtains, the tawdry bits and pieces of lamps, cushions and ornaments that had helped make the cheap little bungalow look like home had been packed away in the waiting barrels that stood about the floor, leaving the room as bare and impersonal as a posting inn waiting room.

Joanna had known at once that something was wrong by the way Colonel Barton sought tensely for the right words. And Elvira had held her hands.

"Why didn't you tell me that Mrs. Martingale had left you and the boy here alone?" he began.

"How did you know?"

"I didn't!" He had been almost savage as he explained that until this morning no one had bothered to mention there might be a connection between the inexplicable absence without leave of his aide, Lieutenant Ordway, and Caroline Martingale. He knew, of course, of the rumor that Ordway had been the cause of young Dalton's suicide, but he had not suspected that she had continued to see him since her husband's death. Until dawn, that is, when Ordway's houseboy had limped into the compound, exhausted from his long trek, and informed him that his master and 'Missee Morn'gate' had been overtaken by bandits in the hills and killed instantly. The boy had escaped only by hiding until the slaughter was over, then quietly emerging and burying the bodies.

By that time, Joanna was white-faced, and the colonel added reproachfully that he must go on from here to young Mrs. Ordway who would, no doubt, have hysterics when she learned that her husband met his death while eloping with another woman.

Joanna had accepted the reprimand, and composed herself.

"Why didn't you tell me she was missing? I could have sent someone to overtake them if you had!"

"I didn't find her note until they had been gone for twelve hours and—could you have stopped her then, Colonel?"

"I suppose not. Young Ordway would have had better sense than head for the mountains," he added bitterly, "if he hadn't had his head addled by that woman. I am sure she directed the trip. Where, for God's sake, were they going?"

"To Rome," Joanna said briefly. She rose and found Caroline's note, and as she placed it into his hands, she added slowly, "She took the passage money, Colonel."

Colonel Barton's mouth tightened. He had no intention of writing a second time for funds to that stiff-rumped lord, whose first missive had been so curt and off-putting, but what to do? The Martingale child would have to return to England, but he couldn't go alone. His mother, in her note, had made him Joanna's responsibility. Which was what he would expect of the stupid woman! The girl couldn't take care of herself, much less the child! And she couldn't remain in India. His wife, Elvira, who sometimes irritated him with her righteousness, had already informed him that in Joanna, they had the making of a 'situation,' and whatever else one might say about her Elvira could recognize a 'situation' before it started. With the men outnumbering the women a hundred to one, it was imperative to get the girl away, and since Lord Arkwright was unalterably opposed to paying her passage, one must pass the hat in the officers' mess and hope that things sorted themselves out when the two reached England. At any rate, there was no time to write Lord Arkwright, and for this the colonel was thankful. With the *Rose of Calcutta's* sailing date a week hence, he must make a decision quickly. No doubt, when he learned the circumstances, his lordship would keep Joanna on to care for Georgie, and if not, his wife had a sister and brother-in-law in London who would befriend the girl.

Just before she fell asleep, Joanna paused for a moment to be thankful for Elvira's relations. They were her bolt-hole, and she intended to keep their existence a secret.

Downstairs, the duchess was indulging in a few well-chosen words of her own.

"I find it impossible to believe, Simon, that that girl is either calculating or wanton! Surely you noticed that garment she was wearing?"

Her nephew managed to smile slightly at the memory of the offending garment.

"That," he commented, holding a glass of wine to the light and eyeing it reflectively, "was the cleverest ploy of all, Aunt Celia. I must admit that when I first saw it, I wondered in what dustbin she found it, but then I realized she had worn it deliberately. It threw us off. It convinced us that she was too poor to buy clothes and must accept secondhand garments. It made her look innocent, charming..."

"Hardly that, I must say," her grace commented dryly.

"Personally, I thought she looked like a little girl playing dress-up, until I saw that she had aimed for precisely that effect," he replied curtly. He shifted restlessly. "I told you, she is clever. That pale, exhausted look—all of it has been assumed for our benefit, Aunt Celia."

"Simon, I don't believe it. Not of that girl. I

could swear she is genuine. Barry Northcote has made some sort of ghastly mistake..."

His lordship shrugged. "A ruse to raise her price. By pretending her blackmail demands are requests for child support, she avoided incriminating herself. You read the colonel's letter. He made no secret of what he thought of her. Would he be so indiscreet as to hint to me that the child was neglected if he had not felt it strongly?"

Her grace continued to look dissatisfied, but she said nothing more.

"She has also been extremely clever about avoiding any direct reference to the Collection, by referring to it coyly as 'saleable merchandise.'"

"How much do you think she'll ask for it?" the duke wondered.

"She'll be a fool if she takes less than twenty thousand pounds."

"Twenty thousand!" Her grace gasped. "The estate can't stand it."

"It can and will, if Miles wants the Collection bad enough."

"I want it," Miles said grimly. "I would like to get it for less, however."

"I admit that I, too, dislike seeing her walk away from us with a fortune in her grasp while she laughs at us."

"I suppose it would be useless to try to ransom her for the Collection?" Miles asked reflectively.

"Oh, I think so. Her partner might abandon her and attempt to market it elsewhere."

"You're talking nonsense!" Her grace's voice held more than a hint of amusement. "You two are talking like a pair of schoolboys! Or highwaymen! Threats! Ransom, indeed! What does this woman want, anyway?"

Lord Arkwright repeated Joanna's words, his voice rigid with loathing. In spite of her regard for his feelings, the duchess found herself laughing.

"What a lot of bother over nothing! It seems to me that a little common sense is needed here. She—Joanna—may have put it a little crudely, but her wants are reasonable—London, clothes, parties, and in the end, I suspect, she would settle for a complaisant husband! What is so wrong with that? Why can't *we* give her what she is seeking? Take her to London, buy her some clothes and introduce her to some eligible men? She will find that she needs our goodwill more than she needs a moldy old Collection. Miles can even offer to provide her with a nice little dowry. The offer will be discreetly publicized, of course, with a few hints dropped in the right places, and who knows? She might even capture a matrimonial prize!"

Miles looked interested. "I think it is an ingenious idea, Mother. It might be the very thing so long as we can keep her from disgracing the name of Martingale. What do you think, Simon? Will she do?"

His cousin had been listening in frowning silence. "I don't like it! What's to prevent her from making a scandal and ruining you, Aunt

Celia? I would rather not have you involved with that woman."

"Stuff!" His aunt said inelegantly. "Joanna make a scandal? I don't believe it! I think you disapprove merely because you didn't think of it yourself. You *know* it is the perfect solution!"

"Will you think so if you find yourself unable to control your guest's behavior?" he asked dryly. "I think you have forgotten that you are extending your hospitality to a product of George Martingale's tutelage."

"I find it easy to forget that when I am with her, Simon," she returned mildly. "Personally, I think the girl will be a credit to me, once she has had a little London polish."

"Are you quite sure you want a guest who might steal the teaspoons?"

"Nonsense, Simon. You make too much of her reputation. As for me, I prefer to trust my own instincts that tell me this girl is basically sound. Of course, if you still insist that she won't do after you and Miles have observed her at dinner tonight, then I shall abide by your decision." Her eyes sparkled mischievously. "But I think you will be surprised at how well she can go on. So why not give my proposal your consideration since you have no other?"

CHAPTER III

JOANNA WAS AROUSED by a discreet tap on the door followed by the entrance of a very superior French maid. She announced herself as Céleste, her grace's dresser, and she carried a gorgeously colored silk shawl over her arm. Joanna found the idea of a maid unnerving, and this elderly Frenchwoman seemed more forbidding than the duchess herself. She did not know that Céleste had been briefed beforehand by her mistress and warned of the impossibility of making anything out of this frumpish little colonial, and was actually looking forward with secret relish to the challenge. However, even Céleste felt a twinge of misgiving as her eyes traveled from the woebegone tearstained face down the full length of that impossible garment.

By the time she had finished, she was beginning to think of herself as a genius. With the garment removed and a pretty muslin dress substituted, Joanna was discovered to have a nice figure. The tanned, brown skin was unfortunate, of course, but at least, the tan was even and the sun-reddened cheeks had not needed any cosmetics. Céleste's deft hands had braided the mass of hair into a simple coronet, and by allowing a few curls to fly at the ears and nape of the neck, she had softened its severity. With the Norwich shawl bringing out the color of Joanna's eyes, Céleste thought her mistress would be well pleased. However, she merely contented herself with an eloquent shrug and discreetly murmured, *"Je ne sais pas, madame,"* when she returned.

Joanna was downstairs well in advance of the dinner hour, hoping to establish herself in a corner before the others appeared, but unfortunately, his lordship was ahead of her. Exquisitely attired in a well-tailored coat of dark blue superfine, pale cream pantaloons and a waterfall of silk at his throat, he paused in the act of pouring himself a glass of wine to raise a surprised eyebrow at her changed appearance.

"Sherry, Mrs. Martingale?" he drawled. "Or perhaps your tipple is something stronger?"

Joanna answered shortly, "Sherry will be fine, my lord." Inwardly, she fumed as his lip curled sardonically.

"Allow me to congratulate you upon the improvement in your appearance, Mrs. Martingale, although I can't say that it is unexpected," he murmured ironically, as he handed her a glass of sherry. "An actress's role is rather difficult to maintain once it stretches beyond a few hours, isn't it?"

Having no idea what he was talking about, Joanna contented herself with "Indeed?" uttered in a suitably bored voice as she cautiously received the glass.

His lordship did not elaborate on his provocative remark and they were soon joined by his aunt and his cousin. The duchess brought with her a slightly warming trend to the hostile atmosphere. She had changed her dress to one of gray satin with a modest neckline and sleeves. Joanna was impressed with its richness, having no idea that her grace considered it her least becoming gown and had deliberately worn it so that she would not outshine Joanna. As for the duke, Joanna found him more approachable than she had expected, although she would have never defined his stiff courtesy as friendliness. However, his fledgling awkwardness reminded her of some of the younger officers in India.

Meantime, his lordship, having seen to his guests, settled himself beside Joanna and proceeded to ruthlessly question her about her past.

"We are curious about your first meeting with George," he began smoothly. "Was it in India, or here in England?"

"It was in India." She calmly sipped her sherry, borrowing freely from the story she had heard Caroline tell. "The Governor General was having a garden party at the palace. All of the bachelor officers were required to show up, and

I was there, also. George met me and..." she allowed her voice to trail off demurely.

"I am sure you were attending as someone's younger sister, and had been allowed to slip in unobserved to see the festivities?"

"Not at all. I was a guest, just as George was. I am aware that you are paying me a compliment by hinting that I look too young to have a child of five, but I assure you that I am older than I look."

"Obviously, you must be." But he did not pursue the question of age. "Surely you were not in India on your own? You must have had parents, a brother, or relative of some sort...?" he paused suggestively.

"My parents died in a plague in India within a day of each other. My father was an army officer and I was their only child, so I have no relatives."

"My dear child. None at all? How frightful!" The warmth of her grace's voice might have been due to the discovery that Joanna's background was respectable enough to include an army officer for a father. "Surely there are relations here in England?"

"No. My Grandfather Marlbern—my father's father—had died, too, in the meantime, and so had my grandmother. Grandfather Marlbern had been a vicar in a small village called Twickford-on-the-Sea in East Anglia, and my father was their only child. My mother," she stirred restlessly, "was Scottish. I know nothing about her family except that her father cast her off when she married an Englishman."

"Perhaps we can locate him, Mrs. Martingale. Would you suggest that we begin our enquiries at Twickford-on-the-Sea?" Lord Arkwright's eyes gleamed mockingly, and she knew he hadn't believed a word that she said. She would not put it past him to do just that, in hopes of finding some discreditable story about her, but if he did, she had nothing to fear.

"You must please yourself," she snapped.

"Oh, be assured that I shall do just that, Mrs. Martingale. Did George ever speak to you of his fixation that he was the true Duke of Somerton?"

Her jaw dropped. "Of course not."

"He never spoke of returning and petitioning the court to be recognized as the rightful heir?"

"Of course not! That—that's insane! Why would he want to do that?"

"He would have to have his cousin declared illegitimate, of course."

"What?" She almost leaped from her chair. All three of them, with their similar faces, were watching her closely. "Then he would have to s-say that y-you..."

"Yes," the duchess said agreeably, as Joanna's eyes sought hers. She was looking slightly amused. "George was slightly mad on the subject of the family succession. You didn't know?"

"N-no."

"That is the reason he wanted the Collection. He thought it would improve his case."

Joanna flushed, embarrassed at the thought of the humiliation these people would suffer when they learned that they had made their frank disclosures to a stranger, rather than a member of the family, as they thought. She shuddered to think of Lord Arkwright's reaction, in particular.

Leaping suddenly and agitatedly to her feet, she begged desperately, "Please don't say anything more. I didn't know—but I understand now why you..." she was going to say "hate me" but substituted instead, "resent me." "If you prefer me to leave this house at once, I will."

"My dear child, of course we would not." Her grace did not seem in the least embarrassed. "I knew you were a nice child, and if you knew anything at all about George's wild ambiions you would repudiate them!" She cast a triumphant glance at Lord Arkwright, who seemed singularly unimpressed by her logic. "We are not so foolish as to blame you for George's bad manners," her grace continued gaily. "You must not be uncomfortable. Try to concentrate on pleasant things. And now, I see that Simon's butler has been trying to tell us that dinner is ready. Shall we go in?"

Thankfully, dinner passed off without any more painful exposure of family secrets. Joanna's mother had instructed her in the elegancies of life, and it was pleasant to be back in her mother's gentle world, no matter for how brief a time. However, Joanna had an unpleasant feeling that she was being watched closely, that everything she did or said was being weighed. Although she replied politely, she had no fund of small talk about Society such as the duchess enjoyed. The names were strange to her; she could do nothing but listen. Then, Lord Arkwright intervened ruthlessly, and carried her further afield in the world of books and poetry. Here, Joanna acquitted herself very well, for she was fond of reading, and if she could have forgotten that she was talking to Lord Arkwright, she would have enjoyed herself. But whenever she looked up, she saw him watching her, wearing what she privately considered his own expression of nasty cynicism.

Finally, after an interminable meal, her grace rose and prepared to leave the gentlemen to their wine. As she was passing her nephew's chair, she paused, and asked, with an uplifted brow: "Well?" His reply was a shrug, and she laughed triumphantly.

Joanna had no time to ponder the exchange, for as soon as they were in the drawing room her grace patted the sofa beside her as she took up her embroidery, and with a sigh Joanna sat down, prepared for a further inquisition.

"Do you like needlework?" her grace asked instead.

"I have not had the opportunity to learn, ma'am. Plain sewing comes easily to me. I make most of Georgie's and my clothes."

A slight look of irritation marred the pretty face. "May I offer a word of advice, my dear?

Remarks of that sort are in bad taste. It is considered boring to parade one's virtues."

"I am sorry, ma'am."

"There, I said you would do," the duchess said approvingly. "Look how prettily you accepted my reproof. And may I congratulate you upon your behavior at the table? Your manners are quite acceptable."

Joanna felt a twinge of amusement. "Thank you. I was trained by my mother in which fork to use, so the compliment, if any, must go to her. You mustn't think I am a barbarian merely because I have lived in India."

"No, of course not." her grace's voice was chilly. She did not enjoy teasing when it was at her expense and moreover, she was not interested in India and still less in Indian manners. "Now, for practical matters. I propose that you spend a few weeks with me as my guest. In London. It is what you said you would like to do."

"Thank you, ma'am," Joanna said uncomfortably. "I don't think I have the proper clothing for that sort of thing, however."

"No, I am sure you do not. So why not allow me to assist you in buying what you need? The city is rather thin of people right now, and I am sure we can get together a wardrobe in time for the Season, which is already upon us. After that, if we continue to enjoy each other's company, I propose that you stay with me and attend some of the events, which will give you an opportunity to meet some people. Do you like the idea of doing so?" She did not see any reason to mention the sordid subject of seeking a husband. Surely, with a woman as clever as this one it was unnecessary.

"You are very kind," Joanna said firmly, in spite of a sudden, urgent longing to do just as the duchess had asked. "I must not intrude upon your hospitality, however."

"Why not?"

"I don't think you really like me, Ma'am," she said bluntly. "I don't understand why you would want to do this for me."

"What an odd thing to say. Do you always make a habit of being rude when someone has offered to do a favor for you?"

Joanna reddened. "No, ma'am. I apologize for my bad manners, but Lord Arkwright left me in no doubt about how you feel toward me. And although you might feel some obligation for Georgie, I cannot see how you can feel any for me."

"My dear child, I do see that you would be reluctant to accept my hospitality if I, like Simon, were not related to you. But my son is the head of your husband's family. He—we—feel a duty, not an obligation, to assume your support. Don't you think you would enjoy a few weeks of gaiety in London before you settle down somewhere with the child?" She smiled coaxingly. "Simon said that is what you wanted, above all things?"

Joanna squirmed, caught on the horns of a dilemma. She would rather forget some of the things she had told Simon, if possible. Of course, her grace expected her to have meant what she said, but her problem was that although Georgie had every right to look to his cousins for protection, she had none. So far, she had accepted nothing from these people, but if she went on with this deception and accepted gifts while masquerading as a Martingale, she would be guilty of a crime. She thought Lord Arkwright would enjoy putting her in prison if—when—he heard about it. She corrected herself hastily, aware that already she had begun to think of putting off her confession for a while. She shuddered with dread. After all, she reminded herself, she could not desert Georgie now, no more than she could afford to draw back at this point. Still, she hesitated, aware of a reluctance to surrender her freedom to become what was, in effect, her grace's pensioner.

Finally, frowning slightly, she asked slowly, "Will his lordship be there, too?"

"Simon?" Her grace seemed surprised by her question. "No. He need not worry you if he should be. My nephew has his own life to lead, and our paths rarely touch. Why?"

"I think Mrs. Martingale would prefer giving London a wide berth if I am to be there." Lord Arkwright strolled into the room, followed by the duke. Joanna wondered how much he had overheard. "I think, after this afternoon, she and I understand one another perfectly. She made her position clear to me, then, just as I would let her feel my wrath if she should abuse that position."

"I do not fear you, Lord Arkwright!" she flashed, unbearably exasperated by his inference that she could not be trusted to behave herself unless she was under his all-seeing eye. She turned swiftly to the duchess. "Thank you for your kind invitation, ma'am. If you still wish me to, I will be glad to go with you tomorrow and be your guest. I find that I cannot get away from Mockridge Hall fast enough!"

CHAPTER IV

THE FOLLOWING MORNING, after a series
of delays, they finally departed. No matter how
short the journey and brief the stay, the duchess
traveled in style, with an additional carriage
to carry her various possessions that were considered absolutely necessary to her comfort
wherever she went, such as her favorite pillows,
eiderdown, her hip-bath, and various other
items that Joanna could only guess at. There
was also another carriage, purloined from her
nephew's stables, and it carried Céleste, Georgie and the nurse she had stolen from her
nephew's domestic staff. It was not that she disliked children, she explained to Joanna, it was
simply that they were not to be borne while
traveling. To be forced to endure their childish
prattle, and perhaps a bout of travel-sickness,
was more than she could tolerate. Although she
did not say so, her grace had never liked her
own children so well until they became adults,
and she found her own daughter, Maria, with

her constant chatter about her two brats, a dead bore.

This, Joanna soon learned, was her grace's second bête noire. She dreaded boredom. And she was counting on the novelty of having Joanna around, dressing her in fashionable clothes and watching her flirtations, to keep that boredom at bay. She was a good-natured woman and so long as it cost her nothing more than money, she was willing to take on the task of sponsoring Joanna, but she naturally expected to enjoy it. Moreover, she felt a slight thrill of triumph at having confounded Simon with her plan and she was determined to prove to him that it could be done. She would show him that Joanna could be pried loose from the Collection for a lot less than twenty thousand pounds! And Joanna was so nice, and grateful and humble, without being toadying, that her grace found herself *liking* her. Granted—she was an opportunist, but her grace could not wholly condemn that in a person, since she had been something of one herself at one time.

She and her twin sister Molly had only been eighteen when they had pulled off the coup of the Season by capturing the two richest matrimonial prizes in London. How teeth had gnashed and rumors had flown! Of course, poor Molly had not lived long to enjoy her position as Lady Arkwright, for she and her husband had been killed in a carriage accident when their infant son was only a few months old. The baby's uncle, the Duke of Somerton, had been appointed his guardian and Simon had grown up at Somerlea, the duke's favorite estate, with his cousin Maria and George. And then, when Simon and Maria were thirteen, and George slightly older, the duke had died. For three months, George had been the triumphant heir until baby Miles was born, the infant Duke of Somerton. All of those people who had shaken their heads over the fortunes of the beautiful O'More twins and alternately envied and commiserated with them, now said that it looked as though Celia had fallen on her feet again, by having a son instead of another daughter. Her grace, therefore, could appreciate Joanna's precarious position.

Her grace was not a woman of great intellect but she knew her own small segment of Society, and as the carriage proceeded toward London, she tried to explain it to Joanna. "Much as I would like to obtain a voucher from Almack's for you, which would automatically open all doors, it is not advisable. Simon thinks George's reputation would prevail against you. He says we must proceed cautiously, make a few friends slowly at first, allowing you to attend a few functions, but not pushing your acquaintance upon anyone. Simon thinks your Martingale connection will carry you, once people learn that you are not some horrid creature George picked up in India. Simon..."

Joanna, who had begun to grow weary of the repeated use of Lord Arkwright's name, interrupted ruthlessly, "His lordship seems to know a great deal about social ostracism. Is it necessary that he order my visit in London?"

"Well," her grace said thoughtfully. "I think we would be wise to be governed by what Simon thinks. I suspect he has gained some experience during his—er—connection with Marjorie Lindsay."

"Marjorie Lindsay?"

"Lady Lindsay, I should say, the widow of Sir Thomas Lindsay, baronet, and a man old enough to be her grandfather," she added ironically. Obviously, her grace did not approve of Lady Lindsay. "She treads a fine line between acceptance and outright ostracism. When Sir Thomas died, she was Lord Carlyle's mistress. There have been half a dozen since then, and she is now living under Simon's protection. Naturally, she no longer has a card for Almack's and the starchiest hostesses cut her dead, but one sees her everywhere, particularly where the hostess is a friend of her current protector."

"I see." Joanna did not escape the inference that her circumstances were the same as the notorious woman's who was Lord Arkwright's mistress. "Is she beautiful?" she asked curiously.

"Ravishing," her grace said briefly. "She hopes to trap Simon into marriage, and sometimes, I think she might succeed, for he is enslaved by her beauty. You should see the matched pair of chestnuts he gave her recently."

The duchess stopped abruptly with that confidence, apparently suddenly becoming aware that she was indulging in gossip about her nephew with a stranger.

London lived up to all of Joanna's expectations, a sprawling, wicked city, with squalor and beauty, povery and great wealth living side by side. As for Somerton House, where she was to spend the next few weeks, it was an imposing old mansion in a fashionable section of London. It was rather gloomy and filled with portraits of forbidding ancestors. The rooms were so vast and the corridors so dark that mere chandeliers could not penetrate the gloom.

Joanna's bedroom was small and cosy, and located very near the set of stairs leading to the nursery where Georgie would be sleeping.

"I would prefer to live in a smaller place," her grace told Joanna frankly. "However, Miles is adamant that we must keep Somerton House. Yet, he hates it as much as I do. He has a great deal of family pride." She sighed. "Look at the absurd way he feels about the Collection."

"Dear ma'am, what is the Collection?" Joanna asked curiously.

The duchess looked at her sharply. "You don't know?"

"No," Joanna said slowly. "I don't know. Should I?"

The duchess laughed shortly. "We thought you did, and had it, or at the very least, knew where it was. To answer your question," she continued, still with that odd look on her face, "the Collection, or more properly, the Saxon Collection, is a set of family heirlooms that has belonged to the head of the house of Martingale since the Norman conquest. It was part of the dowry of a Saxon heiress whom William the Conqueror awarded, along with her land, her serfs and the original timbered manor house of Somerlea, to one of his favoite barons, Jocelyn de Martingale. Family history has it that the Collection belonged to King Arthur."

"And—it is?"

"Composed of five pieces in all—a crown, an armlet, a ring, a drinking cup, and a piece of plate. Gold, of course, and studded with a few precious stones, but of little value to anyone but an antiquities collector—or the Martingale family. I can't understand," she added suspiciously, "why George did not tell you about it. He stole it from Somerlea seven years ago, the night before he departed for India. Miles was only a boy, but he saw him leaving the armory room with a bag in the middle of the night. The following day, by the time we discovered its loss and could make an attempt to regain it, George was on the high seas."

Joanna stared at her blankly. They must think she had it; in fact, Starnes must have been looking for the Collection when he stripped her luggage. "I don't have it," she said quickly. Gold? Gold slipped through George's fingers— he had probably gambled and lost the Collection, long before she came upon the scene, for she had never seen it. "I don't have it, your grace," she repeated. "George must have gambled with it and lost."

To her relief, her grace seemed to accept this, for Joanna had no liking for being thought a thief. No doubt, she would inform her precious nephew, who would, therefore, see how wrong he had been. If Joanna could have read her grace's mind just then, she would have been appalled.

As a matter of fact, her grace had no intention of telling her nephew anything. He and her son were stubborn, blinded-with-prejudice *men,* and they would merely laugh at her instinct which told her that Joanna was telling the truth. As for the Collection itself, she found *that* subject intensely boring. It was for her son to bother with: she had too much to do to worry about a collection of golden objects, in spite of its rumored legends and history. It did occur to her, however, that Simon would think it unnecessary to appease Joanna with a new wardrobe and a husband if he became convinced she knew nothing about it. Therefore, if she wished to continue with her entertaining novelty, she had much better keep quiet about Joanna's confidences. She could soothe her own guilt by not buying *quite* so much as she had originally intended, and perhaps skip a few of the most boring parties.

Beginning from her first morning, when Joanna was called into her grace's bedroom to have her hair cut by a dapper little Frenchman, her week was a whirlwind. He had walked around her with his head cocked before pressing her into a chair and wielding a pair of scissors as though they were a paintbrush and Joanna the canvas. As he snipped, her hair, freed of its own weight, began to curl. Her grace, propped up with lacy pillows in bed, sipping her chocolate, discussed hair styles with him as though Joanna was not present. When he finished, he produced a hand mirror with a hissed *"Voilà!"* Joanna was stunned at the transformation his cunning fingers had made in her appearance. Her hair, gathered into a knot, fell in graceful, curling tendrils around her face and nape.

That haircut set the pace for what followed. Her grace did not bother to consult Joanna about what she preferred but relied upon her own impeccable clothes sense. By the end of the first week in London, she had begun to feel decidedly panicky. The bills were mounting up as she saw, with shocked surprise, the number of gowns her grace considered indispensable for the briefest of stays in town. There were times when she wondered if her grace had any idea of the amount of money she was spending on her. There were endless conferences with the French modiste, Madame LaCotte, where the mysteries of French bead edges, worked jaconet, spider gauze and pearl rosettes with silver fringes were discussed, but Madam apparently considered it vulgar to mention the price of any of the gowns that were being turned out of her workroom by her seamstresses. Occasionally, Joanna overheard the discreetly murmured cost of a bonnet or a dozen pair of white kid gloves, and the cost of these items alone made her blanch. But there were also silk stockings, slippers and half boots, parasols, shawls—the list was endless. Joanna could not even guess at the staggering total of the whole, but when she tried to imagine Lord Arkwright's reaction to his aunt's orgy of spending, she shuddered. She knew that she must call a halt.

Accordingly, she approached her grace during the hour when she was resting before dinner. Giving the briefest of taps, she opened the door and walked in, prepared to encounter some opposition. It was something of a shock, therefore, to find the duchess in the midst of a passionate embrace with a stranger. The gentleman was fully dressed but the lady was wearing a flimsy negligee, and was pink-cheeked and confused by Joanna's unexpected entrance.

"Don't go. You are not *de trop!* It is merely that I haven't seen my dearest Sidney for so long. He has been in the country, and came straight around to see me as soon as he got in town. Come, you may talk to him while I dress."

She rose, by now remarkably composed and unembarrassed, and slipped into her bedroom. By this time, Joanna's face was livid with color. She was not unused to Caroline Martingale entertaining gentlemen in her negligee, but her grace was a lady old enough to be her own mother and she was given no clue from her careless explanation as to the place Lord Sidney had in her life. But he rose and gravely bowed over her hand as though they were meeting in a drawing room.

Lord Sidney was a tall, austere man of middle age, with graying hair and a pair of keen, dark eyes. He was watching her closely with a slight twinkle; and when the duchess left them alone, he plunged straight to the point.

"You have never heard of me, then, my dear?" he asked, smiling slightly.

"No-o, my lord."

"Come, come. You must be wondering if I am Celia's lover, aren't you?"

"It is not my affair, my lord."

"True, but nevertheless, you are entitled to an explanation since you will be living with Celia for some weeks, and there will be times. . . . We have been lovers for eighteen years—it began after her husband's death, I assure you. My wife and I are separated, and since we have no children to draw us together, we rarely see one another. She prefers her gardening and the country, and, like my dear Celia, I prefer a life in town. When my wife wishes to come to London on one of her rare visits, she writes me and I leave her the house and visit my country estate for a few days. It is a very amicable arrangement and it suits us both."

"But, my lord, surely you can get a divorce?" Joanna was embarrassed as soon as the words were out and made an attempt to retrieve them. "I beg your pardon—that was impertinent, but . . ."

"Not at all." He laughed gently. "My wife refuses to grant me one and I cannot force her without a scandal. Scandal would not suit Celia, who would be snubbed by Society and forced to live the life of an exile. So we find it easier to continue as we do."

"Does everyone know?"

His eyes twinkled. "If you mean her children, yes, of course, they know. These things are commonplace, you know. Oh, occasionally, Miles is goaded by Maria into making noises like a son, but when he does, I leave town. Have you decided, because of this, that you disapprove of Celia?" he added.

"I would not presume to do so, my lord," Joanna said firmly. "Her grace has been too good to me, and I like her too much."

"Yet you walked into this room with a decidedly militant air as though you had a complaint to make."

She flushed. "I am very disturbed at how much money her grace is spending on me. I want to call a halt to it. Apart from everything else, Lord Arkwright is going to be very angry when he learns of it."

He looked at her as though she was speaking in a foreign language. "Lord Arkwright? *Simon?* Why should it be any of his business? Celia is a wealthy woman in her own right and she does not have to have her nephew's permission—no, nor her son's neither, to indulge herself by buying you some trinkets."

"Hardly trinkets," Joanna said dryly. "She has a warm heart but she is much too generous."

"My dear child." Lord Sidney took her agitated hands in his. "These bills are nothing, nothing, compared to what she could have spent at the gaming tables this week if she had been bored and lonely. Having you here—buying you some clothes—has amused and entertained her. She has found you a pleasant companion. You must not spoil her generosity, her pleasure, by mentioning the bills. But why are you so worried about Arkwright? Shall I take him to task over his behavior?"

"Please don't!" Joanna said hastily. "It will merely draw his attention to me. Let it alone."

"Are you so afraid of him, then?" He dropped her hands. "Very well. If you say so. But if he complains too much, I will offer to pay your bills myself. That will make him ashamed of his churlishness." He laughed.

Joanna thought it was more likely to make him immediately jump to the conclusion that Lord Sidney had another more personal motive, but she said nothing more. The following afternoon, she had an opportunity to hear for herself Lord Arkwright's reaction to his aunt's shopping. She was joining her grace for tea, and she was wearing her new yellow sarsenet. Her mirror told her that she had never looked more elegant or prettier, but her mood was shattered when, as she approached the drawing room, she overheard that familiar hated voice above the clink of the teacups.

"So the little widow has taken you for all she could get, eh, Aunt Celia?"

"That's ridiculous, Simon. I was not 'taken'

for anything. Actually, the child was most reluctant to accept anything I bought her but I could hardly take her out in public wearing those rags she brought from India."

"Yes," he agreed cynically. "The rags were a nice touch. I only hope you don't regret having given your little puss the claws to scratch you with, Aunt Celia. How did you get around the fact of her mourning, or is it to be ignored altogether?"

"Naturally not! You must know it would be a mistake to lie about her position. As for her widow's weeds, it is not necessary to emphasize her mourning, since no one knows the exact date of George's death. Her first appearance will be in half-mourning, and thereafter, she will be wearing colors. Why should she mourn George, when he was so disagreeable and she looks so pretty in colors?"

There was a burst of mirth at this logic, and Joanna grasped the doorknob and entered just as Lord Arkwright turned away from the window, his face breaking with laughter. The laughter died as his narrowed eyes took in her appearance, an arrested look on his face. His cousin and his aunt were seated before the tea table. There was no sign of Lord Sidney.

Miles rose as she entered and came forward to bow over her hand. "How do you do, Mrs. Martingale?" he said, awkwardly, boyishly. "My mother has been telling us how much she has enjoyed your company this week."

"Thank you, your grace."

"Sit down, my dear," the duchess said graciously. "Have some tea. Now, Simon," she added challengingly, "what do you think? Isn't Joanna's new hairstyle a great improvement?"

Joanna glared at him defiantly as he pretended to inspect her with great deliberation, even to the point of gazing at her through his quizzing glass.

"Vastly so," he drawled. "I confess, I have wondered before this, Mrs. Martingale, why you, a known beauty, have neglected so many of the tools that your sex normally employs to enhance your looks?"

"A known beauty?" she asked sharply. "Why do you call me that?"

He looked surprised. "I was told before your arrival of your beauty."

"Indeed? Who has been talking about me, my lord?"

"Barry Northcote. Surely you remember Lieutenant Northcote, Lord Lindville's younger son. He was a frequent visitor at your house," he added meaningly.

Joanna put down her tea cup with a little click. An image of a boyish face and distressed blue eyes rose to her mind. Lieutenant Northcote had been very angry with Caroline for leading his friend, Lieutenant Dalton, into falling in love with her, then throwing him over for Ordway. The boy had not taken it very well. There had been a scandal when he had committed suicide. No wonder, she thought bitterly, his lordship had been quick to condemn her, thinking she was Mrs. Martingale. Several wild impulses went through her mind, then common sense asserted itself. If Barry Northcote was in London, she had better prepare herself for the truth coming out.

"I remember Lieutenant Northcote," she said in a cool, poised voice. "Am I likely to see him again? It would be a pleasure to talk over old friendships in India with him."

"So far as I know, he is not in London nor likely to be." An unwilling look of admiration flitted across his face. Without taking his eyes off Joanna's face, he asked his aunt, "Shall you be going to the Castlemaine's ball tomorrow night, ma'am?"

"I shall," his aunt said firmly. "Joanna and I met Lady Sophie Castlemaine in the Park yesterday and she was kind enough to extend an invitation to her also."

"However did you manage that, Aunt Celia? Her ladyship has three plain daughters she must launch. She certainly doesn't want to add another pretty girl to the competition."

"Joanna is no competition," her grace replied composedly. "Sophie Castlemaine was quite gracious when she learned her circumstances."

He grinned. "Which you manged to get across while you were merely exchanging civilities in the Park? I congratulate you again, Aunt Celia!"

"I hope that I may count on your presence," she said smoothly. "Sophie said she had sent

85

you a card. She was obviously hoping you would look in. Moreover, I will need you."

He frowned slightly. "You have Miles," he said shortly.

"Miles is a boy, and has absolutely no idea how to fend off Sophie Castlemaine's man-hungry tactics. Whereas you, Simon, you could make Joanna a success simply by standing up with her for one dance. I know the ball will be dull, but you need only look in for a short while."

"The girl is a Martingale, and she has your backing. That should be enough," he replied in a bored voice.

By this time, Joanna had had enough of listening to her grace pander to his lordship's disgusting vanity. She had no intention of sitting quietly any longer while these two discussed her as though she was not even present.

"Your grace," she said crisply. "I would prefer that you cease importuning Lord Arkwright. He is right. I don't need him, and I certainly don't want to be obligated to him for *anything*."

Her grace could not have been any more astonished if the tea table had talked back to her. "What?"

"Lord Arkwright does not like me and I certainly do not like him," she said frostily.

"Well!" Her grace sounded more aggrieved than offended. "You might think of me for a change! I have gone to a great deal of trouble on your behalf, and it seems to me that you would be grateful to *me*. Frankly, Joanna,

George's reputation was not so good that you can afford to be choosey about accepting help, wherever it comes from. As for Simon not liking you," she added blankly, "what has that to do with it? He is not doing it for you, but for me."

Joanna was scarlet with mortification. Her little balloon of independence had been felled with a plop before it hardly got off the ground. Furthermore, she had weakened her position by showing Lord Arkwright her resentment, and a quick glance at his amused face showed that he recognized it.

"I don't care about going to the party," she muttered. "Lady Sophie did not really want me."

"But of course she didn't!" the duchess said patiently, as though explaining to a child. "Haven't I said so? But she dare not leave you out when it means that Miles and perhaps Simon might attend."

"Which is precisely where I came in," Simon said smoothly. "Leave me out of your intrigues, Aunt Celia. If you cannot manage on your own, then you've gotten in over your head."

This last was too much for Joanna. She had no intention of allowing the duchess to *grovel* any longer to this appallingly egotistical man! "Does that mean that we can count on your absence, Lord Arkwright?" she flashed. "Is it possible that I may depend upon it?"

He eyed her enigmatically but his reply showed that he had accepted the gauntlet. "Would you be interested to know where I have been this past week, Mrs. Martingale?" he remarked smoothly, abandoning the subject of the party. "My cousin and I have been talking to the inhabitants of Twickford-on-the-Sea."

"Snooping about, asking questions about me!" she snapped. "Were you able to dig up anything to my discredit, my lord? Or did you find to your disappointment that I had not lied?" She rose abruptly. "If you will excuse me, your grace, I would like to go to my room." As she was leaving, she reflected that Lord Arkwright was chalking up quite a score. This was the second time he had managed to chase her out of the room.

Miles ran her to ground a little later in the library, where she was standing before the shelves looking for a book in the vain hope that a little quiet reading would restore her temper.

"Mrs. Martingale," he said anxiously. "I wanted to correct your impression. My cousin and I were not snooping to find something to your discredit. We hoped to find some trace of your relatives."

With an effort, she managed to speak politely. "And did you?"

"No. But you may be interested to know that your grandfather has recently been making enquiries about you. Your mother's father, I mean."

"No, I am not interested, your grace. He never answered any of her letters, and it is too late for her now. I don't understand someone like that—someone who is prepared to turn his back on his own flesh and blood."

He flushed. "I suppose you mean by that you think I am rather hard on your son?"

She hadn't meant that at all. "That is a matter for your own conscience," she said carefully. "But—he is only a child."

"George's child," he replied, but he was frowning thoughtfully. "What do you think I should do for him?"

Before she could reply, they were interrupted by Lord Arkwright. He was standing in the open doorway, and had apparently overheard most of what they had said. Joanna felt the chill of his disapproval from where she stood.

"It is rather late to be making other arrangements for your son, Mrs. Martingale," he said coldly. "My aunt has gone to a great deal of trouble to give you what you professed to want. I suggest you stick to the original agreement now."

"It wasn't like that, Simon . . ." Miles began.

"Miles, I beg of you, don't interfere with your mother's plans." His sardonic eye took note of Joanna's heightened color. "What about it, Mrs. Martingale?"

"I do not intend to overset her grace's arrangements, Lord Arkwright," she replied coolly.

"Precisely. I knew you would see reason if I pointed out your duty," he replied smoothly. Joanna longed to slap the arrogant smile off that handsome face. "I have a suggestion to make to you, young Miles. How about moving to my house since you intend to remain in town for a few days?"

Miles hesitated.

"I have you booked for a round or two with Gentleman Jim Jackson himself," his cousin added coaxingly. "And I have my eye on the sweetest pair of high-steppers you'll ever see. They come up for auction at Tattersall's next week but if we move fast, we may pick them up before then by private sale. You have been saying you wanted a new pair for your curricle. How about it?"

Miles was caught, hook, line and sinker. "Do you mean it?" he asked excitedly. "Simon, you are willing to take me to Jackson's boxing salon and the Gentleman himself will box with me? He—he only does that with his best customers!"

"Of which I happen to be one. And he is quite willing to oblige me. Then you do want to go?"

"Oh, yes!" The boy's eyes were shining. "I'll have my valet pack my things now. Please wait on me. Don't leave until I get down."

Simon laughed. "I'll wait." He watched smilingly as Miles hurried from the room but when he turned back to her, she saw that he was in the grip of cold anger.

"Hands off the cub, Mrs. Martingale! I won't allow you to sink your claws into him. He is not up to your weight, so look elsewhere for your dalliance, madam."

"How dare you?" she gasped. "As though I would...Oh, you horrid, crude man! Do you think I would...." She stopped as sheer, indignant fury paralyzed her voice. "I think this has gone beyond mere dislike, my lord," she hissed. "You and I hate each other too much for me to stay. It is time I leave here."

"Leave?" His eyes narrowed. "So that is your plan!" he said icily. "And where do you want to go? To Stratford, perhaps?"

"Perhaps," she said stiffly.

"Oh, no—you don't. That offer is no longer open. I shall advise Miles to withdraw it at once."

"I can't be bothered with what you advise!" she spat. "I will go to the duchess and ask her . . ."

"I don't think you will find her receptive to you if I tell her what I suspect."

"And what do you suspect, Lord Arkwright?" she asked scornfully.

"That you have suddenly seen an opportunity to land yourself a very big fish indeed. No less than the Duke of Somerton. He is merely a boy with his milk-teeth hardly cut—but then, you specialize in boys, don't you? A clever little adventuress like you could twist him around your finger if you could get him alone long enough," he added maliciously. "No doubt you are unaware that Miles is a minor and his fortune is subject to his trustees' approval until he is twenty-five. I happen to have been one of his trustees since I attained my majority, and I promise you, Mrs. Martingale, you will not be allowed to destroy Miles as you have others. For one thing, you will not have the chance, and for another, I intend to see that you stay right here in London, where I can keep an eye on you, until you either marry someone else or give up your son's claim upon the Duke of Somerton!"

CHAPTER V

LORD ARKWRIGHT WAS still angry when he arrived at the charming little house he rented in a cul-de-sac off Brook Street, on the fringe of the most fashionable section of the city. He opened the door with his own key and was handing his cloak to the crisply uniformed maid when a soft voice floated to him from upstairs.

"Simon, darling, wherever have you been?"

He looked up and the breath caught in his throat. She was wearing a sheer negligee and nothing else, and was a vision of bewitchment and delight as she posed against the stair-rail. He had unconsciously expected someone like Marjorie Lindsay when he listened to Barry Northcote's cynical description of George Martingale's widow, but nothing could have been further from that brown little termagant than Marjorie, with her ash-blond hair, her soft, white curves and her face of a Botticelli angel. She was not just beautiful; she was the most beautiful woman he had ever seen; and if her soul was that of a courtesan, a man could drown himself in the haunting loveliness of those blue eyes.

As he bounded upstairs and followed her into the bedroom, he thought how much like Marjorie herself were the luxurious furnishings and scented atmosphere of this cosy little love-nest. He was rather surprised at himself for making such a cool appraisal; normally, he was too hot-headed when with her to make an analytical judgment at all.

He had brought along an expensive bauble to reconcile her to his week-long absence, and after receiving her most effusive kisses, he found himself actually breaking away to speak of the subject that was foremost in his mind— his quarrel with Mrs. Martingale. Almost absent-mindedly, he put Marjorie aside and began irritably to tell her of his misadventures. At first, she listened tolerantly, as she preened herself before the mirror and watched the effect of the candlelight on the rubies and sapphires in her new brooch. Then, gradually, as Simon continued to talk, a vague feeling of uneasiness crept over Marjorie. In vain she tried to tell herself that in talking over his worries with her, he was paying her the compliment of treating her as a wife, but it was no part of her plan to have him completely forget her presence— her presence, moreover, seductively clad in the sheerest of negligees—until she *was* his wife.

Marjorie Hartley had been nineteen when she made the observation that mere beauty alone was not going to be enough to catch a rich, titled husband, so she settled for Sir Thomas Lindsay, an immensely wealthy baronet in his sixties. At the time, it seemed her best opportunity to get some of the things in life that had so far been denied her.

There had followed a series of lovers as Marjorie flung herself into a sensuous enjoyment of her new life, free from restrictions and abandoned to the pursuit of pleasure. Marjorie had no intention of spoiling her figure for the sake of bearing a child, so Sir Thomas, seeing his hope of an heir dwindling, and with his eyes opened to his wife's true nature, took his revenge by willing his fortune away from her at his death. Marjorie took the rebuff philosophically. Rather than return to her parents and poverty, she took up a profession that suited her very well—that of a rich man's mistress.

Now, after three years of that life, she was becoming restive. She longed for the security of marriage and respectability, but she had learned her lesson well. She had no intention of again becoming an old man's darling. She wanted a young man, one who would be lover as well as husband, and in Lord Arkwright she had found her ideal mate. He was everything she wanted: thrilling, wealthy, endowed with a vigorous mind, and he was capable of the quixotic gesture of marrying his mistress if he so wished. The censure of the world would not deter him. He would expect an heir, but this time, Marjorie viewed the prospect without her previous horror. She had even toyed with the idea of becoming pregnant to force his hand, and only the fear that he would be so angered by her tactics that she would lose everything prevented her from doing so. So, she wisely continued to appeal to his senses by her lovemaking expertise, and by being available whenever he needed someone to talk to.

Tonight, however, it was not working. After so long an abstinence, the lovemaking should have come first, then the talk. By now, he should have forgotten about that other woman and noticed her enticing body that she had been displaying so liberally for his view. Frustratedly, she dropped beside him on the bed and began to knead his back muscles.

"Darling," she purred seductively, "forget all about that dreadful woman, and think about us. You need your supper and bed."

"I'm not hungry and I'm too keyed up to sleep," he retorted absently.

"That's what I hoped you'd say," she breathed into his ear.

He stood up and eyed her quizzically. "Pray, madam, don't tempt me before I have unclothed myself. I am still wearing my boots and if I followed my present inclinations, I'd tear your sheets."

"Pooh, who cares about the sheets?" she pouted, caressing his thigh.

"Not I," he murmured. Eyes kindling, he flung himself upon the bed, all thoughts of Mrs.

Martingale and pink silk sheets fleeing from his mind.

Afterwards, Marjorie lay back among the pillows in a haze of contentment, well-pleased with her ability to deflect his thoughts from another woman; only to find that his lordship regarded their passionate bout of lovemaking as merely a passing interlude. Hastily, he began to redress himself in the clothes he had stripped off so impetuously an hour earlier. He must return now to his own home, he told her, so as to keep an eye on his young whelp of a cousin who might do something foolish. Most of all, he must keep an eye on Mrs. Martingale, whom he suspected of intriguing against them.

Marjorie was filled with consternation. It was part of her master plan to have his lordship awaken each morning in her bed, and she was conscious of a burning desire to see this woman who continued to occupy his mind when he was with her. She got her wish the following day.

Joanna awakened that morning still angry with Lord Arkwright. If she could have shaken the dust of Somerton House off her feet right then, she would have done so. She brooded over his arrogance, his conceit, his almost brutal disregard of her feelings. In fact, she hated him so intensely that it made her blood bubble merely to think of him, and she wanted nothing so much as to do him an injury. Her mind dwelt pleasurably on the thought of such Gothic horrors as thumbscrews, boiling oil and the like, before coming down to earth and reviewing the perils of her situation. And Georgie's.

She had only a few shillings, not even enough to find a lodging for the night, and certainly not enough to keep herself until she could find a situation. And what situation could she—a lone woman—find, that would include a child? Reluctantly, she came to the conclusion that she must leave Georgie behind when she went, and hope that perhaps, once she was settled as a governess or nursemaid, the duke would allow her to see him occasionally. Meantime, the sooner she saw Letitia Witherspoon, and made arrangements to leave, the better. She did not know that worthy lady, but Elvira had assured her of a haven with her sister.

The Witherspoon knocker was answered that morning by a neatly dressed housemaid, who seemed astonished to discover a modish young woman upon the doorstep, alone, apparently having been conveyed by the hansom cab that was fast disappearing down the street. Joanna's bronze-green walking dress of Italian crepe with its matching bonnet of twilled velvet proclaimed her stylishness, and it was precisely that incongruity that had the housemaid confused, for the Witherspoon family did not number fashionable young women among their acquaintances. However, she answered Joanna's query very pleasantly, and eyed her curiously when she saw her dismay at learning that the Witherspoons were in the country right now.

"You're surely not going to walk, miss?" she cried when Joanna turned away.

"Why not?"

"It won't do, miss. Let me get you another cab."

Joanna smiled. "Thank you but I will be all right. I know the way back to—er—my home. Goodbye."

If it had been Calcutta, Joanna would have thought twice about entering its busy streets alone, but this was London, and she did know the general direction in which she had to go. The Witherspoons lived in a solid middle-class neighborhood of merchants, barristers and physicians, and although the way back to the Somerton mansion in a more fashionable area of town led her through the tip of Bond Street and a part of Oxford Street, she saw no difficulty in negotiating it. But most importantly, Joanna had so little money that she could not afford the luxury of a cab. It was a paradox that Joanna wore a fortune in clothing on her back and dined off gold plates, yet she had less money than any of the servants in her grace's house.

It was not until she reached Oxford Street that she realized that she had made a mistake. Perhaps if she had not stopped the ginger-haired man in the plaid waistcoat to ask her way she would not have had any difficulty, but she was surprised when he took her enquiry as a personal invitation to accompany her. At first, she informed him civilly that she did not need any further assistance, and then, as he continued to walk beside her, talking, she fell into a cold, snubbing silence. He was not daunted. Finally, she stopped and faced him angrily.

"See here, if you don't leave me alone, I shall ask the first gentleman I see to knock you down."

His small, gimlet eyes narrowed to slits. "Try it, my doxy, and see 'ow far you git!" he jeered. "A liddy wouldn't be walking the streets alone, an' I know it! If it's the brass you're worried about, I've enough in me pockets to meet your price."

Joanna looked about desperately. They were attracting some unpleasant attention, but everyone was hurrying past with their heads averted, unwilling to be involved. Suddenly, as welcome as rain upon a parched desert, a familiar, mocking voice fell upon her ear, a voice that only that morning she had wished never to hear again.

"May I be of assistance, Mrs. Martingale?"

"Oh, my lord! I am so glad to see you!" Her exclamation of heartfelt relief brought an oddly quizzical look to his face.

He quickly stepped from an open barouche that had pulled to a halt beside them at the curb. Joanna gained a confused impression of another person in it as his lordship removed his hat and bowed before extending a gloved hand to help her up the steps.

"You must be desperate indeed to welcome *my* help so eagerly," he murmured.

Joanna said nothing but the convulsive way

she gripped his hand spoke for itself. Like magic, her tormentor had vanished. Belatedly, she realized that the other occupant of the barouche was another woman, and even before the introductions were made, she knew that she must be Lady Marjorie Lindsay. Her beauty proclaimed that fact. She was dressed so as to dramatically highlight her fairness, in black, with a string of priceless pearls around her throat and a pair of pearl drops in her ears. The sensuous sheen of black silk was a foil for her glowing, camellia skin. Joanna wondered if Simon was responsible for the pearls as well as the ring on the ungloved hand the lady had resting on a white ermine muff. Seeing that Joanna had noticed it, Marjorie pointedly tilted her hand.

Marjorie's cold blue eyes traveled slowly over her rival. Last night, desperate for reassurance that he was not falling in love with another woman, she had extracted a promise from him to return to her this morning so they might go to her favorite jeweler in Bond Street. Once there, he had paid with bored resignation for the expensive ring she had chosen. She had been triumphant, seeing the ring as a demonstration of her power over him. She had been too insensitive to appreciate the cynicism with which he had listened to her enraptured thanks.

Now, she wondered why she had been so foolish as to worry about Mrs. Martingale. True, she was elegantly dressed, but she could not approach *her* beauty. Simon was sure to notice the contrast as they sat side by side. She smiled at him meaningfully, but he was watching Mrs. Martingale.

"I could have easily missed you, you know," he said irritably. "If you must walk the streets, then you should be accompanied by a maid. Otherwise, you leave yourself wide open to that sort of insult. That man can be pardoned for thinking you welcomed his advances when..."

"I didn't!" she interrupted defiantly.

He eyed her smolderingly. "Whatever possessed you to be this far from home, alone and on foot?"

Joanna thought grimly that fate had played her a dirty trick by making Simon her rescuer. Why couldn't it have been Miles—or Lord Sidney? And as usual, he was taking advantage of her predicament to scold her. She was not blind to the covert amusement of the lady beside her, who was drinking in his words eagerly.

"I cannot see that it is any of your business, Lord Arkwright," she replied frigidly, "but if you must know, I was visiting a friend—who was not at home—and I lost my way."

He raised his eyebrows. "I was not aware that you had any friends in London."

"And I was not aware that I was accountable to you for every move I make!"

"Why did you not borrow her grace's carriage for your errand?"

This was beginning to sound like an inquisition. Joanna's voice grew colder. "She was going to use it herself. I took a cab, my lord, but it was such a fine day that I thought I would walk home."

"And now you have learned that you made a mistake," he retorted disagreeably. "The very least you could have done, if you contemplated such an action, was to take a maid. But perhaps you did not care to have a witness to your—er—tryst? Is that why you won't give me the name of your friend? Do you prefer to sacrifice your reputation in order to protect him?"

Joanna scowled furiously at him. How dare he make an insinuation like that? How dare he humiliate her in the presence of his mistress? How could he infer that her reputation was ruined, merely because of a thoughtless action on her part when this woman who was listening so avidly had no reputation to lose? By chastising her in Lady Marjorie's presence, he subtly inferred that of the two, Joanna's character was in doubt. Marjorie, meanwhile, titillated by Joanna's discomfort and Simon's heedless words, unwisely took a hand in the conversation.

"Perhaps Mrs. Martingale is unaware of our customs, Simon," she purred. "She has been in India where the ladies are freer in their ways. My dear Mrs. Martingale, you must never go out unaccompanied in London. I myself never do. It leads to a certain misapprehension about one's morals."

No doubt Simon thought her words sweetly reasonable but Joanna heard the malice in her voice and felt the kittenish claws beneath the soft white sheaths. She exploded. She was damned if she'd let Lord Arkwright's mistress lecture *her* on her morals!

"In your ladyship's case, it is vital that there be no misapprehension about your morals," she said silkily, "but in mine, I can assure you, I have no reason to advertise."

She was pleased to see a deep flush overspread Marjorie's face.

"I think you owe Lady Marjorie an apology, Mrs. Martingale," Simon said slowly. "I can't believe that you were unaware of your implication."

"I am glad to see that you credit me with the intelligence to know what I am saying, my lord," she replied evenly. "Like Lady Marjorie, I spoke with the express intention of offending. It was unkind, however, and I apologize for that. I know you wish to be rid of my presence. Since we are near Somerton House, perhaps you will set me down now."

Marjorie inclined her head rigidly without speaking.

"We'll both get out here," Simon said abruptly, calling to the coachman.

"Simon, no!" Marjorie clutched his hand. "Don't leave me to go home alone. Come with me. I demand that you not leave me!"

His lips tightened but he said nothing, merely dropped his aloof gaze to her clutching fingers until she reluctantly released his hand.

"I'll see you later," he added casually, stepping from the barouche. He gripped Joanna's arm with remorseless fingers. "Do you always say what you think?" he added furiously.

"Let me go!" She struggled to pull loose. "I apologized," she snapped. "But it was not her place to lecture me—nor yours!"

"She was trying to be helpful!" he gritted."She has been married, and knows something of London ways. You are a girl who has lived all your life out of this country."

"I have been married, too, remember?" she cried triumphantly.

Obviously, he had not, for he was taken aback. "Even so," he said warily, "you should be told when you forget your manners."

"I should not!" she hissed in a goaded voice. "Not by you! I am not your mistress, Lord Arkwright!"

"Indeed?" he drawled, his eyes narrowed as they inspected her flushed, angry face. "May I say that your crudity never ceases to amaze me, Mrs. Martingale? Perhaps I have been given a clue to what is at the root of our misunderstandings? If so, I can easily do something about remedying the disappointment you apparently feel."

She whitened. "You—I..." The malicious twinkle in his eyes stopped her embarrassed stammering. "You are a beast, Lord Arkwright! I hate you! I—I have had enough of your v-veiled insinuations..."

"I was not under the impression that they were veiled."

Before she could reply to that provocative remark, they were hailed from the street. His grace, resplendent in a new coat and Hessian boots, was pulling his curricle to a halt beside them. He looked as though he was barely suppressing some strong emotion.

"May I speak to you alone, Simon?"

"Of course." Simon disengaged his arm from Joanna's and added menacingly, "Don't attempt to walk on alone, Mrs. Martingale."

They moved out of earshot. Once or twice, Miles's voice rose excitedly, and once Joanna thought she heard her name. She knew they had been talking about her when Simon returned, for he was angry and wasn't bothering to hide it.

"What were you saying about me?" she asked bluntly.

"My cousin had an odd encounter with an Indian gentleman this morning. Do you know any Indians in London, Mrs. Martingale?"

"No."

"Not that he is really an Indian. Miles suspects that he was an Englishman in disguise. He may have even been a onetime crony of George's," he added significantly.

"Indeed?" Joanna said shortly. "Then, no doubt, he had something discreditable to say about me?"

"Why should you jump to that conclusion, Mrs. Martingale?" he asked silkily.

"Well." She was taken aback. "You said he was a onetime friend of George's. Why should he approach his grace, unless he wishes to blackmail him? About me?"

"Oddly enough, he had something to sell, but it was not information, Mrs. Martingale." And then, as she stared at him blankly, he added smoothly, "I find your thought process most revealing. From crony—not friend—of George's to blackmail, is most interesting. Could it be that you have a guilty secret on your conscience?" By this time, they had halted before the doorway of Somerton House. "Remember, you are not to walk unaccompanied on the street. If you will not accept Lady Marjorie's word for it—or mine—ask her grace. She will tell you it simply isn't done—by a lady," he added blandly.

CHAPTER VI

JOANNA HAD A quivery, butterflies-in-the-stomach feeling about tonight. Her first ball, and she expected to be a social disaster, or at the very best, a wall-flower sitting among the dowagers, never getting a single request for a dance. George's reputation and her own ineptness would ruin it for her. Why else had it seemed so important to the duchess to have Simon present, and why had he refused? Of them all, he had known the truth: she was gauche, a social nonentity. So her thoughts ran, as she stared at herself in the mirror and tried to summon her courage while a funny little knot of stubbornness would not allow her to cave in. She might not be a beauty like Marjorie Lindsay, but she was no antidote either. She was going to show his lordship that the success of her first ball did not depend upon him!

She knew that she was looking exceptionally well, partly due to the dress—her first ball dress, a shimmering gray that was worn under an overskirt of spangled gauze that the duchess had chosen to mark her half-mourning. Céleste had done striking things for her eyes, darkening the lashes with burnt cork until they looked silvery and mysterious, and touching her lips with the merest suggestion of the pink salve the duchess used regularly.

As she descended the stairs, where the duchess awaited her with Miles, their startled eyes told her the truth. In a surprised, pleased voice, the duchess said, "My dear, you are a credit to me tonight! No one would ever guess that you were a widow with a five-year-old son. Not that you can afford to deny it," she added, sighing, before going on to a more pleasant thought. "That gray was an inspiration."

Miles said nothing but his stiff, self-conscious manner told Joanna, who had developed a sensitivity to snubs over the years, that he had been warned—possibly that she was a mantrap, and therefore to be avoided. He was so coldly withdrawn that his attitude finally reached his mother, who asked him crisply after they were settled in the carriage, "I hope you're not sickening or something, Miles?"

He denied it embarrassedly and she added, "Well, we don't want to get your contagion if you are. It would be disastrous for Joanna to come down with a putrid sore throat or some such thing."

He promised that he was not falling prey to sickness, and to Joanna's relief the subject was allowed to drop.

Lord and Lady Castlemaine and the oldest of their three plain daughters were receiving the guests. They were greeted with cries of pleasure by her ladyship but Joanna, who had become cynical in a week's time, knew that *her* welcome was due to Miles. They were not allowed to move on until Lady Castlemaine had wrung a promise from him that he would dance at least once with each of her daughters.

The ballroom, glittering with light, overheated, smelling strongly of perfumed flowers, was overflowing with beautifully dressed people, or so it seemed to Joanna. However, her grace, after one critical glance, remarked disparagingly, "The room seems rather thin of company, doesn't it? Well, it's to be expected. The Castlemaines have never been famed for their hospitality. The food is bound to be skimpy, the punch watered, the music inadequate and the hosts are such paragons of respectability that everyone avoids them." Joanna did not miss the inference that but for her her grace would have avoided them, also.

Her first dance was promised to Miles. It was a country dance, and involved little touching but some standing together. Refusing to act like a dullard without saying a word for thirty minutes, Joanna began to talk brightly, and after the first few hesitant replies, Miles forgot his wariness enough to venture a few stammering remarks of his own. By the end of the dance, he was even smiling slightly. For a girl who was attending her first ball, and was fearful of being a wallflower, it was equivalent to being belle of the ball.

To her delight, Lord Sidney was waiting with her grace when Miles returned her to where his mother sat among the chaperones. He arose at once, as soon as they appeared, and gallantly requested the next dance. It was to be a waltz, his lordship informed her, and she must ask one of the patronesses of Almack's for permission before she danced it.

"Didn't the duchess warn you?" he added, offering his arm.

"Yes, my lord, but I don't know any of the patronesses."

He frowned slightly. "That shall be remedied at once," he said promptly. "I see one of them standing over there. Mrs. Drummond, the starchiest of them all, but a great favorite of mine. Come. I'll introduce you to her."

Mrs. Drummond regarded her with a frown. "Staying with Somerton, you say? That's odd. Celia has not requested a voucher for her."

"No," Lord Sidney agreed. "Mrs. Martingale is the widow of an officer who was in His Majesty's Forces in India. She has a small son and is totally dependent upon Somerton. Her circumstances being what they were, her grace did not think she should place any of you in the embarrassing position of having to refuse a voucher until Mrs. Martingale had been in town a little longer."

Mrs. Drummond's face cleared. "Nonsense," she said approvingly. "I understand Celia's hesitancy, but if Mrs. Martingale's birth is as good as her marriage to a Martingale, then she should have a voucher, dependent widow or not. Tell Celia to see me about it." And she nodded her agreement as the musicians struck the first waltz.

"See how easy it is," Lord Sidney laughed as he led her onto the floor.

"Except, my lord, I have never learned to waltz."

He looked surprised. "Indeed? I thought they were waltz-mad in India. However, you are in luck that I am to be your first instructor," he added teasingly. "I am very proficient at teaching young ladies their steps. First, we get off on the sidelines, out of the way of the more polished dancers, and you merely listen to the music and follow my lead. My hand at your waist will guide you as to where you should go."

At the end of the dance, Lord Sidney told Joanna that she had acquitted herself very creditably. As they were returning to the duchess, who was deep in conversation with a strange gentleman, he added, "I want you to save me another dance."

Dear man, she thought, I know you would rather not dance at all, unless it is with your Celia, but thank you!

However, in her absence, Lady Castlemaine had not been idle. She had brought a partner for Joanna, whom she suspected would be monopolizing the duke's time tonight unless she did something about it. Her 'something' was Sir Humphrey Mayhew.

Sir Humphrey was in his mid-thirties, with a slightly portly figure and a solemn face. He was the only son of a widowed mother who lived with him on his Derbyshire estate. He had recently been left a tidy fortune by an uncle in the West Indies, and upon returning from there had announced his decision that it was time he took a wife. Lady Mayhew was thrown into disorder, and while she was recovering, Sir Humphrey took himself to London to see what the Season had to offer.

He did not think of himself as a vain man, but he was aware that he was a good catch for some lucky girl, and he intended to make the best match he could for himself. He had looked the field over tonight, passed completely over the three Castlemaine girls who had been pushed hopefully into his path, and made the discovery that the only girl who appealed to him was waltzing with Lord Sidney. From Mrs. Drummond, he had learned her name and something of her circumstances, and from Lady Castlemaine, an introduction to her chaperone.

He put his cards on the table, so to speak, at once with the duchess, and she, thrilled that Joanna had only been out 'on the town' for less than an hour and had already made a conquest, gave her own censored version of her circumstances. She was pleased to see that he was not put off by the news of Georgie, particularly after she made some allusions to the child's expectations. Gleefully, she envisioned Simon's consternation when she told him of her triumph. So much, she thought, with a mental snap of her fingers, for Simon's dour predictions of disaster!

She greeted Joanna's return with a gracious recommendation of Sir Humphrey as a partner, and added vaguely that he had recently returned from her part of the world.

The dance was a cotillion. Joanna, who had the impression that he was shy, asked kindly, "So you have recently visited India, Sir Humphrey?"

He looked blank. "Not India. The West Indies." He went on to describe the vegetation of the islands in detail. She soon realized that botany was his hobby, and she found that all she had to do was provide an occasional nod or smile to keep him going.

He led her to the punch-bowl after the dance, and brought her a claret cup. Then the mask that she had thought was shyness dropped.

"The dowager duchess informed me that your son is the heir to the Duke of Somerton?"

"Yes." She was slightly startled. Heretofore, it had not seemed that any of the Somerton clan had relished acknowledging it.

"The duke is young and will no doubt eventually have sons of his own," he went on briskly. "Nevertheless, I understand he has every intention of providing handsomely for the boy's future?"

He did? Joanna thought. She replied coldly, "I have never asked the duke his intentions."

Sir Humphrey was unsnubbable. With a tight smile, he deplored her laxity, but agreed "that would be the business of your husband."

"I am not married, Sir Humphrey," she reminded him shortly.

"I should say, your future husband." There was no mistaking his significant smile as he prepared to lead her back to the duchess. However, once there, instead of moving on, he remained, teetering on his heels and continuing his monologue, this time on the beauties and advantages of his estate in Derbyshire. Even her grace was put out of countenance. Weighed against his obvious eligibility was the possibility that he could destroy any chance Joanna might have of meeting another, more desirable suitor. There was no help from Miles either; he had disappeared. Looking around desperately, she suddenly spied Simon.

He was standing near the door talking to a good-looking young man with the erect bearing of a soldier. His brown hair was sun-streaked and he was tanned a healthy bronze. Simon saw them, too, and recognizing his aunt's wiggling eyebrows as a plea for help, he seized his companion's arm and started toward them just as the musicians struck up another waltz.

Joanna was given about four seconds' warning, then Lord Arkwright was bowing over her hand and saying, in a manner that showed his appreciation of her predicament, "Your servant,

Mrs. Martingale. May I present an old friend of yours? I am sure you remember Lieutenant Northcote?"

"Joanna?" the young man said blankly. "What are you doing here?"

Joanna stood up abruptly and grasped his arm. "Barry!" she cried in a high-pitched, unnatural voice. "Barry Northcote! How marvelous to see you again! Thank you, yes, I *would* love this waltz!" And before young Lieutenant Northcote realized what was happening, she had literally swung him onto the floor, her last glimpse of the startled little group a dizzying view of Lord Arkwright's white, angry face.

"Don't say a word!" she hissed. "For God's sake, Barry, you must help me! They are watching us. Smile! Act as though you are pleased to see me."

Barry took a firmer grip on her waist and essayed a tentative smile. "But I am glad to see you, Joanna," he said plaintively. "I had no idea you were in England, but I am delighted that you are. And here, of all places. In a silver ball dress, waltzing." A real smile lit his face. "You'll have to forgive me for sounding so stunned, but I thought I was going to have to meet Mrs. Martingale and..." His steps faltered. "My God, he did say you were Mrs. Martingale! What did he mean? 'Fess up, young Jo, what has that selfish woman gotten you into now?"

"Oh, Barry," she said simply, "I am in the most frightful jam and you must help me."

"You know I'll help you, Jo, but I won't lift a finger to help Caroline Martingale. What is it all about?"

"I am pretending to be her—Caroline. Everyone—Lord Arkwright, the Duke of Somerton, his mother—think that I am her. Even Mrs. Drummond and the whole of Lord Castlemaine's guests think my name is Joanna Martingale, and that I am George Martingale's widow."

He whistled softly. "You are in deep, my dear. If you're not doing this for her, then she'll have your scalp for impersonating her. And why should you want to, anyway? You are a much nicer person than Caroline Martingale, and as for being a widow, if you must, why pick on George? He wasn't a very nice person either! Why claim a disagreeable person like him for a husband?"

"Oh, you don't understand," Joanna cried despairingly, "and I really haven't time to explain it properly because when this waltz is finished, Lord Arkwright is going to come straight over to us and. . . . Oh, Barry, it is so mixed up! In the first place, Caroline is dead. She and Lieutenant Ordway were killed by hill bandits four weeks ago! They were eloping to Rome."

"Good God! Ordway dead! And Mrs. Martingale, too?" He automatically continued to dance as he absorbed what she had said. His face gradually assumed its healthy hue. Joanna watched him anxiously. Finally, "But why are you pretending to be Caroline, Joanna?"

"It was the only way I could keep Georgie," she explained. "You see, when I arrived, Lord Arkwright assumed that I was Mrs. Martingale for he had not been told that she was dead. So, I—I— j-just let him go on thinking that, for I found out that none of them wanted Georgie."

"Nonsense, you must be mistaken, Jo. He is a nice little chap."

"No, it's true, Barry. They don't want him. You forget that he is George Martingale's son."

It was proof of how George Martingale had been regarded by his fellow officers that this explanation was enough for Barry Northcote. "Poor little fellow," he said with easy sympathy. "It's a shame. But, dash it, Jo, you can't pretend to be that woman. You know her reputation. And Arkwright knows all about her. Why, I myself told him..." he stopped, biting his lips.

"I know what you told him, and what he thinks of her," Joanna said patiently.

"I can't have him thinking that you... that is, I'll have to explain." Northcote sounded agitated. "What can he be thinking right now? I profess to dislike you; in fact, I tell him the most disgusting facts about you, then I waltz off with you in my arms..."

Joanna gurgled. "He probably thinks I am practicing my wiles on you. He already believes I am a hussy who can't keep her claws off every man she meets."

Northcote looked appalled. "If he does, it's because I told him so! It is a damned shame, Jo! I'll have to clear this up."

"You can't," she said firmly. "Unless you tell him the truth, and I forbid you to do that! He won't believe you now, anyway. He'll merely assume I've added you to my list of victims."

"I was always one of your victims, young Jo. Even when you were at the Martingales, at the beck and call of that she-devil, I thought you were sweet and pretty. And now, seeing you here in that ball dress, all silvery and beautiful—well, I—I am stunned."

Once, those words would have thrilled her through and through, coming from Barry, but now, she merely regarded him with the tolerant affection of a sister. "I love my dress," she smiled. "I think I shall always remember this night for the rest of my life."

"What are you talking about?" The music had stopped but he retained his grip on her waist. "I am not giving you up now! Not now that I've found you again. I intend to call on you tomorrow—I'll make up some story to satisfy Arkwright..."

"Here he comes," Joanna said in a low voice.

Lord Arkwright's face had regained its normal hue but his eyes were glittering with rage.

"Congratulations, Mrs. Martingale," he said softly. "You may add another victim to your list. You have made another conquest."

Joanna raised her nose in the air. "Somehow, I knew those would be your first words, Lord Arkwright."

"Indeed? I am gratified that I haven't disappointed you. I wasn't prepared for your fast thinking. You got to this young man before I could stop you. I presume you have explained everything to his satisfaction?" he added, still in that soft, menacing voice.

Joanna looked sideways at Barry and giggled. "Of course! But then Lieutenant Northcote and I are old friends."

"Is that true?" Lord Arkwright turned a cold flash of blue toward young Northcote.

Lieutenant Northcote looked miserable and shuffled his feet nervously. "I—er—that is, I was mistaken about some of the things I told you, sir. I seemed to have gotten Jo and someone else mixed up ..."

"Do you think me a fool?" Lord Arkwright broke in icily. "Don't compound your error by making that mistake! It is obvious what has happened! I find that I must congratulate Mrs. Martingale again. I made the mistake of under-estimating her, of course, but I shan't do so again." He bowed slightly and turning, walked steadily out of the room.

CHAPTER VII

FROM THE MOMENT that Lord Arkwright turned and left her, his eyes glittering with rage, Joanna began to enjoy the ball. It was a heady feeling to score a triumph over the arrogant Lord Arkwright: admittedly, it did something for her ego. She regretted having put Barry into a predicament, and she hoped he could pass it off casually as a case of mistaken identity. However, Barry had not much hope of convincing his lordship of such a weak story. He had not wanted to repeat what he knew about the Martingales; he had done so at Lord Arkwright's urging, his very reluctance one of the most convincing parts of his story. It would be impossible to say now that it had all been a mistake. However, with the use of a little judicious evasive tactics, he hoped to avoid his lordship in the future.

The rest of the night was a success, salvaged from what had begun as a disaster. Joanna was not even troubled overmuch by Sir Humphrey, since he was too proper to stand up with her more than twice in one evening. Barry mustered a relief force of young fellow officers who filled her dance program and vied for the honor of taking her to supper. It was heady stuff for a girl attending her first ball.

The duchess was not pleased nor did she approve of Joanna's behavior the following days. Lieutenant Northcote was too frequent a visitor, and although he was usually accompanied by a friend, and his attitude toward Joanna almost brotherly, her grace was perturbed. No one, so far, could come up to Sir Humphrey in solidity or worth, not even Barry Northcote. When it came to a pinch, not many men were going to be willing to take on another man's child, and she wondered if Joanna had forgotten that that was the main issue. Could she possibly think that, because Barry was the son of Lord Lindville, his prospects were as good as Sir Humphrey's, even if Lord Lindville would be so remiss as to allow his son to be entrapped by a widow with questionable morals?

With a view, therefore, to bringing Joanna to her senses, her grace arranged a theater party, inviting Sir Humphrey and Lord Sidney as her only guests. Joanna spent her time evading a proposal from Sir Humphrey, and for the first time, realized how anxious the duchess was to accomplish just the opposite; how eagerly she wished to be rid of her. It was an unpleasant shock.

Whatever may have happened, it was averted

the following morning when disaster descended upon them in the person of her grace's daughter, Lady Houghton. Her ladyship, accompanied by her lord and master and their two children, Master Robert and Mistress Emmaline, as well as a retinue of servants, including her maid and his valet, his lordship's secretary, the children's nanny and Mistress Emmaline's governess, arrived before breakfast. When her grace looked out the window and saw the carriages, all of them piled high with baggage indicating a prolonged stay, she moaned and took to her bed.

Maria was a matronly young woman who had had the good fortune to secure a husband considered to be extremely eligible by all wordly standards. As a girl, she had been large, awkward and plain, but a duke's daughter does not lack for suitors. Lady Maria chose from among the best of them. Lord Houghton was wealthy and well-born, but the fact that he was also dull allowed Maria, for the first time in her life, to occupy the center of the stage.

As Lady Houghton, Maria came into her own. When not occupied with producing Houghton progeny, she had reorganized her husband's estates and meddled into the lives of his servants, his tenants and the villagers, with all the zeal of a missionary. Her motives were excellent but in short order she succeeded in alienating most of the citizenry of the county, although her hereditary insularity as a duke's daughter prevented her from comprehending her offense. If at times she felt that she had not received the gratitude that was her due, she comforted herself with the thought that gratitude came hard for some.

At least once a year she favored her mother with a visit, where she indulged her scope for meddling by criticizing her mother's extravagant habits, her circle of friends and Lord Sidney. The latter usually left town during her stay, and Maria failed to see that her visits made her mother unhappy. Indeed, she sometimes felt injured that her efforts on her mother's behalf went largely unappreciated.

Lord Houghton, who immersed himself in business affairs when they came to London, justified their visits with the comfortable assurance that Maria's periodic interventions were necessary to prevent the dowager duchess from committing some hopeless folly. Therefore, when a troubling rumor reached his wife that her grace was being victimized by George Martingale's widow, he lost no time in leaving for London. Their early morning arrival, after an uncomfortable night spent at an inn on the outskirts of the city, was attended by a great deal of disorder and bustle.

Questioning the servants before she saw her mother, Maria learned that matters were even worse than she had been led to expect: no one had mentioned a child. She swept majestically into her mother's bedroom, armed with this additional item of information, and the battle was on.

Joanna first learned of it when she was vigorously awakened by Céleste and summoned to her grace's bedside, where she found her grace sitting upright in bed, still in her nightcap while she wept gustily into a handkerchief and Céleste held a vinaigrette beneath her nose.

"One of her friends saw us. It could have been anyone, for she has spies everywhere, but it was probably that horrid creature, Fanny Linington, whom I saw peeking at us while we were behind the curtain at Madame LaCotte's. You know, it was when you were trying on that ivory straw satin with the worked brown braid—if you remember, I said it wouldn't do, it was simply too immodest for someone in your circumstances?" When Joanna nodded, she went on, "Wicked creature! She is one of Maria's favorite correspondents and keeps her informed of all I do!"

Joanna privately thought it was disloyal of Maria to have a correspondent who spied on her own mother.

"I told her what a dear girl you are, Joanna, and you are, you know, my dear. Obliging and even-tempered, and always ready to accomodate yourself to my plans without making a fuss or being obtrusive in any way. Very much more satisfactory than my own daughter, I might add. The servants all adore you; even Céleste here, has a kind word to say about you. That is more than I can say for Maria. She asked me if Simon had any idea what was going on, as though there was some deep plot afoot to smuggle you into the house and keep your identity a secret from Simon! I told her that so far as I was concerned, one would never guess that you had ever been married to George Martingale, and she was a trifle mizzled when I told her that, furthermore, Simon knew all about you! But the real shocker was when I told her that Simon had promised me to give a ball for you!"

Joanna sat down abruptly and stared at her grace in consternation.

"But Simon is not my keeper, and neither is Miles nor that odious husband of hers!" Her grace blew her nose vigorously. "He is a crashing bore. Houghton, I mean. Even my best friends avoid him whenever possible. The Prince Regent himself has told me many times, 'Celia, if it weren't for you and Sidney, I'd give that fellow no more than a civil nod in passing, for he's the dullest dog in Christendom.' In fact, Prinny told me that he has never known a man whose conversation could empty a room quicker than Houghton's." Her grace was looking brighter as she dwelled pleasurably on the shortcomings of her daughter's husband.

Joanna felt obliged to offer timidly, "Shall I leave your house, then, ma'am?"

"*No!*" Her grace pulled herself upright, thrusting aside the vinaigrette impatiently. A look faintly reminiscent of her son at his most mulish appeared on her face. "No, absolutely not! If anyone goes it shall be Maria, for this is *my* home, or my son's, and if he does not disapprove of you being here than it can be none of her business. Maria will be careful what she says to Miles, for he doesn't allow her to tell him what to do."

Joanna was moved by this unexpected defense. She had thought her grace did not like her and last night had suspected she was plotting to be rid of her. She was ashamed of her ungenerous thoughts and touched by her grace's loyalty. She had no wish to drive a wedge between mother and daughter, however, and thought it behooved her to smooth down the duchess's ruffled feathers. This she attempted to do by presenting Maria's motives in the most favorable light possible, but she was by no means successful. Finally, Joanna left her grace settled among her pillows, sipping lukewarm chocolate and plotting her daughter's discomfiture.

Joanna was troubled, but she diplomatically removed herself from the bedroom floor to avoid an unexpected encounter. Upstairs, she found the two Houghton children already installed in the schoolroom, with a starched nanny in charge. Georgie's nurse, who had never aspired to any postion higher than a second floor housemaid at Mockridge Hall, had been put to work scrubbing down walls and shelves. Georgie had already turned over the ancient, dog-eared nursery toys to Mistress Emmaline, who was a holy terror and a chip off the old block, and he and little Robert were playing in a corner. Deciding not to disturb the uneasy peace, Joanna slipped away and went downstairs to find Lady Houghton.

She found Lord and Lady Houghton eating breakfast, his lordship with the financial section of the newspaper open and propped against the coffee pot. Maria's face was puffy and ugly from weeping, a pitiful contrast to her mother's lovely, tear-drenched eyes. To give Maria credit, she had feared and hated George Martingale until she was thirteen, when her little brother's birth had put an end to his reign of terror. She had been horrified to hear that her mother was giving his widow a home, and she had hurried to London with the best of intentions, expecting to have to wrest her silly little mother from the clutches of some coarse, brassy creature. Her mother, instead of appreciating her efforts, had taken umbrage and answered back with a few home truths about Maria herself. She attributed this unexpected defiance to the influence of that Martingale woman. Joanna's appearance was therefore a shock.

In her turn, Joanna took great pains to be conciliatory, and was so successful that by the time breakfast was over Maria was beginning to look her old, haughty, domineering self. Until then, Lord Houghton's sole contribution to the conversaton had been a grunt when he was introduced and a surly request for the cream pot, but as they arose, a sort of unspoken communication flowed between him and his wife, and he suggested affably that they move to the morning room where they could talk further. Whether he expected to talk, or allow his wife to do it for him, Joanna was never to know, for just then the butler announced that Sir Humphrey Mayhew had called, and had been put into the morning room.

If Sir Humphrey was taken aback to discover three people instead of one meeting him in the morning room, he controlled his surprise and seemed delighted to meet some more of Mrs. Martingale's connections. When he learned that he was being presented to Lord and Lady Houghton, he pronounced himself overwhelmed with the honor.

"This is indeed a great privilege! I knew, of course, that Mrs. Martingale was living here and was in the habit of accompanying her grace to social functions, but I was not sure precisely what her position in this house was. She could have been here merely as a paid companion to her grace. It would not have been an unlikely situation for a young widow in her position, and her grace might still have shown great condescension by making me personally known to Mrs. Martingale. However, I was granted the pleasure of a few minutes alone with her grace when I first made her acquaintance, and I learned that such was not the case. In fact, her grace assured me that his grace the duke intended to do something handsome for Mrs. Martingale's child, who is his heir. I regretted the necessity of pursuing the matter that closely, but Mrs. Martingale's position was somewhat ambiguous, and one does have one's own name to think of, not to mention the need, on my part, to put the case fairly before my mother. My mind has been set to rest by discovering you here this morning, treating this lady with a degree of complaisance, toleration—familiarity, even—that bodes well for any connection I might choose to make in this direction. I am extremely gratified."

He beamed at one and all impartially. Maria, who had been overwhelmed by his effusiveness at first, suddenly saw a reason for her mother's championship of Joanna, purchasing her a wardrobe and taking her out socially. From the beginning, of course, Maria had known that her brother was obligated to provide financially for George's widow and child. Custom, family opinion and his own pride demanded it. But no one could expect him to install them in his own home, and it had been this that had brought her posthaste to London. Now, all was explained. Her jealousy vanished. She saw now what her mother had seen: the ideal solution was to find the widow a husband, the child a father.

She was impressed with Sir Humphrey. She thought Joanna had made an admirable choice. Here was a discerning man, one who had the judgment to be humble in the presence of superiors. He was impressed by his future wife's connections (as he should be), and obviously, he was affluent. She did not condemn him for his concern over Georgie's financial welfare; any sensible man would be the same. Apparently, all that was needed now was a slight push from Joanna's titled relations.

She said earnestly, "Mrs. Martingale is living

here as my mother's guest, I assure you, Sir Humphrey. Although I have known her only a short time, I have already discovered her disposition to be sweet and compliant."

Sir Humphrey smirked. Mistaking the dazed look on Joanna's face as dazzlement at the broad hints he had given, he said pompously, "I cannot tell you how much your good opinion of her means to me. Of course, my lord, your fame precedes you. I have heard it rumored that you are destined for a high position of statesmanship in the affairs of this country—no, no, I won't allow you to make light of it!—and it gratifies me a great deal to be connected to such an illustrious family. I have heard of your good lady's charitable works in her own home county. You know Mrs. Pennyfeather, of course, my lady? She is a good friend of my mother's. In fact, the two ladies drink tea together every afternoon while they are in Bath enjoying the waters. I have met her many times while visiting my mother there, and she has always spoken of you with the highest regard."

The mystery was solved. Lord Houghton, who was a bore but no fool, might be exasperated by the fulsome compliments, but his lady was highly gratified. It was manna to her starved soul to hear that there existed someone who appreciated her efforts, and Sir Humphrey had been the one to tell her so. It is rare that two people were ever so much in accord as those two were at that moment. Maria positively ached with the urge to do something for him in return.

"My dear Sir Humphrey," she gushed. "Please put your own mind—and your dear mother's—at rest. Mrs. Martingale may have been left in reduced circumstances, but she has a claim on all of us for our sympathy and support. And I think I may speak for all of us when I assure you that her choice will have our full approval," she added archly. "In fact, Mrs. Martingale is in quite a respectable position when it comes to making a decision about her future."

Sir Humphrey was not offended by this plain speaking. "Better and better," he said genially. "My mother will be pleased. I am pleased. I am not seeking a dowered wife; in fact, it is of less importance than a feeling of mutual sympathy and attraction, and here, I might add, I find Mrs. Martingale and myself extraordinarily in accord. However, one likes to have the monetary matters settled, particularly when there is a child involved. I am sure that his grace and I can get down to a talk at a later date. Meanwhile, do you think that her grace would consider me too precipitate if I were to ask Mrs. Martingale to go for a walk in Hyde Park this morning?" All too clearly, one could see what the subject of the walk would be, and Joanna wondered that he would consider it necessary, under the circumstances.

"Not at all," Maria said graciously. "I know my mother will be pleased to agree. It is a beautiful day." For the first time, she looked at Joanna.

Joanna's initial impulse was to burst into

angry speech but she bit it back hastily. A rising tide of hysterical laughter bubbled in her throat, although there was nothing funny about her present situation. In fact, there was something a little frightening about Sir Humphrey's bland self-assurance and Maria's equally arrogant certainty, and she had the uneasy feeling that between them she might find herself betrothed, if not married, if she was not careful.

Before she could speak, the butler entered, followed by Lieutenant Northcote, the Duke of Somerton and Lord Arkwright. They had arrived simultaneously, and had met upon the steps. The latter two had not known the Houghtons were in London, and during the bustle of greetings, Joanna managed to signal Barry warningly.

"How prompt you are, Barry!" she cried at the first opportunity. "If you will excuse me for a few minutes, I will change so that we may go to the Park as I promised you. I am so sorry, Sir Humphrey," she added apologetically, "but I cannot accept your invitation. As you see, I have a previous engagement with Lieutenant Northcote."

Then she fled. It was a tactical error. She discovered that when she returned to the room ten minutes later, dressed for an outing in the Park. While she was gone, it had not taken Simon long to root out the cause of her panic, which had been obvious to him. A few coy remarks from Maria, following a smirking agreement from Sir Humphrey, had given his lordship a clear idea of what was afoot. It did not take him half a minute to take Sir Humphrey's measure and he knew, even if Maria did not, that this man would never appeal to Joanna Martingale. He had a shrewd idea of Sir Humphrey's roughshod tactics, however, and hoped that they, allied with Maria's, might prove so strong that little Mrs. Martingale would soon have her back to the wall. His aunt's scheme, which he had never approved of, would be scuttled at the outset. The situation, meanwhile, was not without its amusing side, so he set to work perversely to baulk Joanna. When she returned, it was to find Simon suavely in charge. He arose and with a bow, indicated a chair for her, while he informed her of their change of plans. Her stroll with Barry had suddenly grown into an outing.

"If you will be so obliging as to wait, Mrs. Martingale, for Maria to change into walking clothes, we will all go together. It seems that Sir Humphrey was so disappointed that she took pity on him and we have arranged to make up a party to walk in the Park. Lieutenant Northcote has kindly agreed to share you with us. I hope that is all right with you?" he added with an ironical glint. "It is, isn't it, Mrs. Martingale?" he persisted gently.

Joanna saw the fine Italian hand of Lord Arkwright, not Lady Houghton, in these new arrangements, but not for the world would she let him see her anger. "It sounds delightful," she said sweetly.

Barry avoided meeting her eyes and she was granted no opportunity to speak privately with him until they arrived at Hyde Park, which was filled with strolling couples enjoying the fine morning.

Under cover of descending from the carriage, she hissed, "Why, Barry?"

"Sorry, Jo," he muttered in her ear. "I was outflanked and outmanouvered from the beginning. His lordship advanced from the rear before I could summon a delaying action." His voice held a ghost of laughter.

Maria graciously told her brother's coachman that he might walk the horses while they strolled. They were six, an awkward number for the park paths, and Joanna was expecting Simon to make some outrageous move. Sir Humphrey had shown an unexpected obstinacy about leaving Joanna to walk with Barry, having been made suspicious by their whispered conference, so when his lordship looked around and as though suddenly struck by a thought remarked, "It looks as though we're going to have to break into smaller groups," she was waiting for him.

Clinging to Barry's arm with a grip born of desperation, and under cover of pointing out to him a rare species of bird that she claimed to see flying overhead, she talked over Simon's attempts to pair her off with Sir Humphrey. Finally, frustrated by Joanna's brilliant spate of conversation and her apparent deafness to his instructions, he despatched Sir Humphrey with a crisp authority that startled even that insensitive gentleman, and remained behind to accompany Barry and Joanna himself. By this time, Barry was shaking with silent laughter and plunged abruptly into the bushes, presumably to examine further the flora and fauna of the Park.

Joanna turned sweetly to his lordship, and apologized prettily for her inattention. "You must forgive me for my enthusiasm, my lord. You must understand that I am interested in learning everything that I can about the vegetation of England. Having lived so long in India, I am naturally ignorant of much about my native land."

Barry, who had returned, almost plunged again at the look upon Simon's face. However, Simon received the remark with every appearance of believing it, beyond a slight twitch of the lips. "But of course. I would have thought, however, that you would have found Sir Humphrey more knowledgeable as a teacher. As I remember, he was lecturing my aunt quite brilliantly on botany at the Castlemaine ball. But then, of course, you were waltzing with Lieutenant Northcote." Having taken the battle straight into the enemy camp, he added, "Incidentally, I believe I cut you off abruptly that night, Lieutenant Northcote. If you remember, you were about to explain to me how you had mistakenly given me false information about Mrs. Martingale—er—I won't sully the lady's ears by repeating it—and I did not allow you to finish. You said you had been mistaken, having confused her identity with someone else's. I am not sure I understand just what you mean."

"I—er—" Barry began haltingly, but Joanna intervened swiftly.

"A poor choice of words, my lord," she said blandly. "Barry meant that your knowledge of me was confused! In other words, you misunderstood everything he told you. I explained it all while we were dancing, and he was appalled to learn that he had given you the wrong impression through some careless words on his part. He wishes you to forgive him for his distortion. He never intended for you to think what you obviously did think."

"Is that true?" Simon asked Barry.

"Ah—yes, my lord," Barry said miserably.

"I am impressed," Simon commented gently. "May I congratulate you, Lieutenant Northcote, upon your admirable explanation? Earlier, I *was* confused, I confess. Now, you have made it all clear. Knowing how embarrassing it is to admit that one is wrong, I think it is generous of you to accept the blame for my mistake. After all, it was I who misinterpreted what you told me."

Barry swallowed nervously and tugged at his shirt points.

"You are too kind, my lord," Joanna said, tilting her nose loftily. "You are very generous to accept Barry's apology so freely."

"Why not? He made it so well," his lordship murmured plaintively.

Desperate to change the subject, Joanna plunged. "My lord, is it true? Her grace told me this morning that you were planning to give a ball?"

His eyes narrowed. "Yes. That is true."

"I must ask you to reconsider your decision if it is not too late and the invitations have not already been despatched. My plans are too uncertain. I—I may not be here. I cannot stay with her grace indefinitely, you know."

"I am not sure that I understand your meaning." His voice was as smooth as cream. "Can it be that you are under the impression that you are to be the guest of honor at my ball?"

"Y-yes. H-her g-grace said . . ." she began falteringly.

"My aunt romances too much. No, Mrs. Martingale, the ball has nothing to do with you. One might just as well say that it is being given to ease—er—Lady Lindsay's way into Society," he added blandly. "For of course, she will be there, too."

"Oh." Joanna said in a chastened voice, having been thoroughly snubbed for her impertinence.

As for Simon, he was looking more cheerful, his eyes noting with satisfaction the hectic flush of embarrassment on her cheeks. By this time, they had come upon the others, who had been stopped upon the path to be greeted by some acquaintances, a young lady and gentleman accompanied by a grim-looking chaperone. The gentleman was Barry's brother, Arthur, who was his father's heir. He bore a strong resemblance to Barry, but lacked the military erectness of his younger brother. The girl was a sprightly blonde with a mobile, monkey face and a wide smile. They were talking to Miles and the girl seemed to know him well. When she turned to see the newcomers, however, she greeted Simon with a crow of delight.

"Simon! Just the lad I want to see! Miles says he is staying with you, and you two have made plans for tonight. Do let him off, or better still come with him. I am making up a party for supper at Vauxhall Gardens and I need you two. Eligible men are always in demand!" She laughed. "I know that makes you want to run the other way, but I shan't let you off. Do say you'll come," she coaxed.

Simon's eyes had softened. "You are a designing young lady, Annabelle. Miles is free to make whatever plans he likes, but I do not think I can."

"Nonsense! Uncle Marcus and Margaret will be there. It will be her first outing since the baby." Her eyes appraised Joanna with frank curiosity, then passed on to Barry. They widened. "Barry Northcote! Where did you come from? Arthur, why didn't you tell me your brother was in town?"

"Why should I?" grinned Arthur.

Barry drew Joanna forward. "Joanna, this rash young lady is Annabelle Maulbrais. Annabelle, may I present Joanna—er—Martingale? She is at present staying with the Duchess

141

of Somerton. She is—er—a—a widow, with a small son," he added, self-consciously. He was uncomfortably aware of Simon's sharp eyes as he stumbled over the lies.

Annabelle blinked, obviously surprised by Barry's information, but she smiled warmly at Joanna. Under cover of the general conversation, she asked, "Have you been staying with her grace long?"

"Not long," Joanna replied. "I have been living in India."

"Then you're a stranger here? And not a recent widow, apparently?" She eyed Joanna's smoky-blue walking dress measuringly.

"No," Joanna murmured awkwardly.

"Good!" Annabelle was a young lady who was prone to make lightning decisions, consulting no one's wishes but her own. "Then you can come to my party also. You will receive an invitation by messenger, but meantime you are invited."

Joanna smiled, slightly taken aback by the abrupt command. Before she could open her mouth to speak, however, they were interrupted by Sir Humphrey, who had edged his way around the circle until he was standing behind her.

"Er—harumph! Your supper party sounds delightful, Miss Maulbrais. I have had the privilege of meeting your uncle, Mr. Marcus Salterson, and I am sure that any party given by him and his delightful wife cannot help but be a success and a pleasure to all those who are so honored as to receive an invitation. May I say that I find myself envying Mrs. Martingale?"

Annabelle's jaw dropped. She had noticed the long, drooping face hovering behind Mrs. Martingale but she had left him out of her calculations. She had thought him a friend of Miles's sister, Maria, whom she considered as belonging to an older generation. She had never been approached with a blatant bid for an invitation before in her life and in spite of her easy address, nothing so far in her training had prepared her for depressing someone who was apparently blind to ordinary social convention. She looked helplessly at Simon, who was wearing an extraordinarily alert expression of amusement.

"You must forgive Sir Humphrey's impetuousness, Annabelle," he said guilelessly. "He has been carried away by his admiration of Mrs. Martingale. The thought of her, and the delights of your party, made him speak without thinking."

Sir Humphrey beamed. "Just so, my lord. You comprehend my motives well. One might also add that I am jealous of all those who will spend an evening in her company."

Annabelle rolled droll eyes at Simon, quizzing him. He was one of a small clique of her uncle's best friends and when he nodded, she gave in gracefully.

"But of course, Sir Humphrey, in that case, you must come, too."

Joanna opened her mouth, then closed it

again, for she saw that Simon was waiting for her to lodge a protest. His eyes narrowed appreciatively as a bright blush stained her cheeks. This was his doing, she thought angrily. How readily, even eagerly, he seemed prepared to turn her over to Sir Humphrey! She made up her mind then. She had no intention of attending Annabelle's party and providing his lordship with any more amusement at her expense.

CHAPTER VIII

JOANNA FOUND HERSELF unexpectedly aided in her decision by the duchess. As late as this morning, her grace would have recommended Sir Humphrey as a suitable husband, but her feelings underwent an abrupt reversal when she learned that he had won Maria's wholehearted approval.

Upon her return from the Park, Lady Houghton had thought it politic to tender the olive branch by showing her mother that she was in agreement with her scheme to marry off Joanna. However, when she entered her grace's boudoir and found her alone, sealing a hot-pressed, agitated note to Lord Sidney, she was guided by her own ill-fated star to say all the wrong things.

"The girl is a taking little thing," she admitted condescendingly, "and I have no doubt that she was ill-used by George Martingale before he married her. But the fact remains that we don't want her sort of person here, and the sooner she is out of this house, the better." Her grace stiffened. "I was very much pleased with Sir Humphrey Mayhew," Maria added graciously. "In fact, you couldn't have chosen a better husband for her. He will soon stamp George's nonsense out of her and be an admirable influence for the boy. It will take a strong-minded man like Sir Humphrey to eradicate any unpleasant tendencies the child inherited from George. Fortunately, too, Sir Humphrey does not lack the means to take care of them, if Miles can be brought to do his part. In fact, it is Miles's duty, and I shall insist upon it. After all, Sir Humphrey must have something to sweeten the pot when he is asked to marry a woman about whom he knows absolutely nothing."

"I was not under the impression that anyone is asking him anything of the sort," the duchess said frigidly.

Maria, who was a totally unimaginative woman, failed to catch the nuance of reserve in her mother's voice. "Really, mama," she said indulgently, "surely even *you* understand that Sir Humphrey must go back to his mother and explain the girl's position to her. If I do say so myself, I think it was seeing that Houghton and I were members of her family that tipped the scales for him. Sir Humphrey admires Houghton very much, you know," she added complacently. "But even so, we cannot guarantee her breeding to Sir Humphrey."

"Her grandfather was a vicar," her grace remarked distantly.

"So Simon told me. But what is a vicar? A country parson!" Maria shrugged. "And how far does that go, if her mother was a shopkeeper's daughter? No, Mama, just be thankful I arrived in time to prevent you from making some awful mistake, such as foisting Joanna off on some impressionable lad like Barry Northcote, for instance. Imagine how embarrassing it would be for Houghton to have to explain to Lord Lindville how his son came to make a mésalliance under this roof!"

"I hardly think it would be Houghton's place to explain anything," her grace commented dryly. "Lieutenant Northcote met Joanna while they were both in India, not here, under your brother's roof."

"But Miles is a minor," Maria reminded her with a patronizing air that set her mother's teeth on edge. "Lindville would naturally hold Houghton responsible for whatever happens in this house."

Her grace, who thought of herself as a mild-mannered woman, was conscious of a flash of pure rage. Who, she thought angrily, did Maria think she was talking to? A fool? She was the Dowager Duchess of Somerton, who happened to take precedent over a mere Lady Houghton, and she was far more conversant with what was acceptable in polite society than either Maria or that odious husband of hers. She had never been a snob, either, and she found herself irritated by Maria's toplofty dismissal of Joanna's antecedents. She thought of reminding her daughter that she herself had not been considered good enough for the Duke of Somerton when she married into the haughty Martingale clan. And where, she thought sardonically, did that leave Maria? George's mother, for instance, a vicious old *grande dame,* had referred to her as 'the pretentious little Irish upstart.' Come to think of it, at times Maria reminded her of Cousin Hortense.

At one time or another, her grace had thought all these things presently being said about Joanna, but it was quite another thing to hear them from Maria. The truth was that her grace's opinion of Joanna had undergone a gradual change. She had, in fact, become fond of the girl and although she felt disloyal to admit it even to herself she did not like Maria very much. And when Maria spoke of Sir Humphrey stamping 'George's nonsense' out of her by making her into another person, her grace had the uncomfortable feeling that he would do his best to make her into someone like Maria herself.

"You may assure Houghton that he will not have to make an apology to Lord Lindville on my behalf," she told Maria icily. "Joanna has no romantic feelings about young Northcote, nor he about her. They are merely friends. As for Sir Humphrey, she won't have *him!* She can do much better. After seeing the way she conducted herself at the Castlemaine ball, I predict she will make a brilliant marriage before the

Season is out." With a great deal of satisfaction, she saw that that had hit its mark.

"Surely, Mama, you aren't condoning—*flirting?*" Maria asked repressively.

Her grace thought irritably, and not for the first time, that her daughter was not only dull but a nitwit in the bargain.

"Why not? How, pray, do you think I caught your father? Fortunately, you never had to use your wits to catch a husband, Maria, but then not all of us start out in life as a duke's daughter," she added maliciously.

"There are times when I think Houghton is right," Maria replied in a mortified voice. "He says you are utterly incapable of managing your own affairs, and I believe him."

"Houghton presumably wishes to manage them for me?" her grace asked sweetly.

Maria reddened. "Not at all, Mama. But we cannot help but observe that at times you think like a girl of twenty, rather than a woman who will not see her fiftieth birthday again. As for George's widow, I think you will see that she has more common sense than to allow a man like Sir Humphrey to slip away, although I am surprised that a man of his intelligence and— and social address wishes to waste his time on a nobody like her when he can do so much better and look higher for a wife. He is wealthy, with far-flung interests in the West Indies..."

"Then he'd better seek his wife there!" snapped her grace. "If you think he is such a good catch, why don't you line him up with one of *your* spinster friends? You have many. Fanny Linington, for instance, would appreciate your efforts," she added guilelessly. "She has certainly been looking hard enough these past fifteen years."

Maria flounced out, leaving her grace with the pleasant feeling of having had the last word.

Joanna was astonished at the change in the climate when she pleaded a headache as an excuse to escape the Vauxhall party that noght. After having Sir Humphrey pushed on her all week, it was a relief to realize that she had wronged her grace by suspecting her of matchmaking.

"I would not have you offend the Saltersons, but I am afraid that Sir Humphrey is becoming a little too particular in his attentions," she remarked piously to Joanna. "It simply won't do to be always in his company unless you intend to marry him—and you don't, do you?" Her eyes sought Joanna's.

"No, ma'am. I—I don't. I cannot love him."

Her grace nodded. "I thought as much. Then there is nothing more to be said. You'll stay at home and allow Simon to entertain him in your stead. It is no more than he deserves after encouraging Annabelle to invite him!" Joanna joined her chuckling at the picture of Simon being forced to endure an evening in Sir Humphrey's company.

The next morning, Sir Humphrey, having been thwarted by his lady's absence the night before, presented himself at an early hour at

Somerton House. This time, he was determined not to be put off. He was lucky enough to find Joanna and Lady Houghton alone, and the latter was willing to oblige him by immediately excusing herself. Joanna recognized the signs of an imminent proposal with a sinking heart. She was trapped, so she resigned herself to listening with as much grace as possible, intending to put her refusal in as kind a manner as she could. However, as she listened, she found it hard to remember that he deserved any consideration. He did not speak of loving her, but he had much to say about her good fortune in having captured his heart, particularly after his misgivings about her suitability.

When he finally paused, she said quickly, "Sir Humphrey, I am conscious of the honor you have done me by asking me to be your wife, but I must refuse. I cannot marry you."

He took that rebuff with a calm smile. "Naturally, you are reluctant to believe in your good fortune, and you are perhaps thinking I might grow to regret having married you. But I assure you, Mrs. Martingale, I have given the matter careful consideration, and have come to the conclusion that I will be quite content to have you as my wife. You may, therefore, accept with a clear conscience that all my scruples have been overcome."

"You are so kind, sir, to reassure me," she said steadily, "but nevertheless, it won't do. I cannot marry you." She hesitated to use the word 'love,' since he had not.

"I understand your playfulness," he said jocularly. "All young women, no matter how eager they may be, must show a reluctance to accept when first made an offer of marriage."

"Indeed, it is not playfulness, Sir Humphrey," she said earnestly, "but I do mean what I say. Please do not make me a second offer because you think I expect it."

His smile broadened. "You may be assured that I will not disappoint you by taking you at your word. I am not such a faint-heart that I will become cast down merely because I have been given a negative answer the first time. I recognize that your pride will not allow you to accept me immediately, and believe me, I admire you for it."

"I have no wish to prize a second offer from you, sir. Please believe what I say. My first answer was my final one. Please do not continue."

He frowned slightly. "If I had not been assured by the ladies of my acquaintance that no woman worthy of being courted allows herself to give an affirmative answer the first time, I might be inclined to think of myself as a rejected suitor. Fortunately, I have been told that the current mode is for the lady to 'play hard to get.' However, it might be well for you to understand your position thoroughly. You are not a maiden making her first bow to Society with a loving, generous father at your back. You are a widow with a child to support, totally dependent upon relatives. Relatives, I might add, who have shown themselves most receptive to my suit. I have the greatest admiration for your character and integrity but—is it possible that you think you will get a better offer than mine?"

She was almost in tears. "I know that I will not. Please, why can't you accept what I have said? I simply do not love you, Sir Humphrey!"

His face froze with distaste. "That is an emotion better left to the lower classes," he said firmly. "I believe you are still suffering from a touch of last night's headache. Meanwhile, I have no intention of taking you at your word until you have had an opportunity to think over your good fortune. You need a period of rest and repose to do so; otherwise, it bodes ill for our future."

With a jerky bow, he withdrew, exuding disapproval.

Joanna had no intention of accepting any man's proposal so long as she was assuming another woman's identity. Unwillingly, Simon's sardonic face intruded upon her thoughts, and she wished yet again that her unruly tongue had not run away with itself at their first meeting. Not that it would make any difference to him, she reminded herself astringently. Nursemaid Joanna Marlbern or Joanna Martingale, widow, she was still despised and distrusted.

That afternoon, Joanna borrowed the use of the duchess's carriage to pay another visit to the Witherspoon house. The same housemaid answered the door and informed her that her mistress and the children were remaining in the country for a prolonged stay. The master had returned to the city, but was at work. This time, Joanna asked permission to leave a letter to be forwarded, and scribbled a message to Letitia Witherspoon, asking for her help.

On the way home, Joanna thought of Elvira Barton, Letitia's sister, that staunch upholder of morals. What would she advise her to do? Unhesitatingly, the answer came. Tell the truth, of course, and relieve the duchess of the embarrassment of her presence as soon and as painlessly as possible.

There was no opportunity that day but the following morning, she sought out the duchess. She found her in her boudoir, her morning's mail scattered about her. She was dressed in something pink that threw a rosy reflection upon her face, and she looked so pretty and so pleased with her life that Joanna's heart almost misgave her.

"My dear Joanna," she began happily. "Now that you have definitely decided against Sir Humphrey—did I tell you that the dear man told Maria that he was returning to his home in Derbyshire to give you time to return to your senses? Anway, now that *that* is settled, it is time we got down to some real work." Her eyes sparkled. "I have here a personal note from Lucy Feversham asking us to a picnic at Lacy Manor on the 22nd. And she adds 'bring your lovely house guest with you.' How is your calendar?"

"Dear ma'am." Joanna sat down opposite her

and took a firm hold on the conversation. "I must confess to something, and please, if you can forgive me, I will be thankful for the rest of my life."

"Indeed?" Her grace smiled slightly. "That sounds most ominous. Pray proceed."

Joanna unburdened herself of her story, starting from the beginning, when she had been left as a young girl in the care of Caroline Martingale on through her death and until the end, when she was unwisely goaded into assuming Caroline's identity.

The duchess had an extremely odd look on her face when Joanna finished, but she merely said, "Dear me, so you aren't George's wife after all. Or anyone's." Her eyes appraised the girl shrewdly. "Most interesting. I must tell Sidney. He was quite positive that you weren't, and it seems that he was right. A most astute observation on his part. But how very strange of Simon to miss it! I wonder why?"

"His lordship and I—did not like one another," Joanna explained wretchedly.

"Yes, I noticed that," her grace remarked dryly. A ghost of a twinkle lit her eyes.

"I know that I was wrong—but I—I was *so* angry . . ."

"Oh, as to that—if we all behaved according to a strict moral code, then the world would be a very dull place indeed. Full of Marias and Sir Humphreys." She shuddered delicately, her eyes now definitely twinkling, and Joanna gave a reluctant laugh. "Does Simon know anything about this?"

"Oh, no, ma'am! I'd die if I—I had to tell Lord Arkwright! Please don't let him know until I have gone."

"Are you planning to go then?"

"Why, y-yes, ma'am. I—didn't think you would want me to stay now."

"Oh, I wouldn't say that." Her grace was brisk. "I do see that you will have to curtail your activities until this matter of your identity is cleared up, but I don't think you should be so precipitate about leaving at once. You are doing no one any harm by staying on as George's widow. Barry Northcote knows the truth, and fortunately, you have no desire to marry Sir Humphrey, so he needs no explanation from you. So that leaves the rest of us— and Simon." She tapped her quizzing glass thoughtfully against her cheek. "Let's leave things as they are for now. Of course, that ban doesn't include Simon's ball."

"I can't attend the ball, your grace. I thought you said..."

"Oh, but this ball you *must* attend. If you did not, Simon would suspect something and we don't want that. You see, I wheedled him into having it for your sake."

Joanna stared at her blankly. "I asked him. I asked him and he assured me that it was not."

"Oh, is that what he allowed you to think?" A trace of amusement flitted across her grace's face. "Oh, no, my dear, this is a ball you must attend. Afterwards, I promise you, we will make a clean breast of all your sins and confess the whole!" Her eyes sparkled. "But first, there is a ball. I do find that I am quite looking forward to it!"

CHAPTER IX

AS THE EVE of the ball approached, rumors began to filter through to the duchess, via the servant's grapevine, about its preparations. It had begun to sound as though it was going to be a huge, garish affair that would be talked about for weeks to come. It was as though Lord Arkwright, having been chivied into it, intended taking his revenge by making it vulgar and ostentatious. It was to be a costume ball, and hundreds of invitations had been issued, extra servants hired from the agencies to handle the serving of the food and wine, and flowers ordered to be distributed throughout the house, with a bower to be erected in the ballroom. Her grace grew more indignant as time passed, and his lordship told her nothing of his plans. Finally, she managed to trap Miles as he came home one morning to escape the confusion, and in the presence of his sister and Joanna, she questioned him about it. Before he realized it, his tongue slipped and he confessed that Marjorie Lindsay was overseeing the preparations.

Her grace was furious. "That woman will take this to be as good as a proposal! She'll see that everyone hears of it! She'll have Simon shackled and on the way to the altar before the month is out!"

"Oh, I think not." Miles, who knew a great deal more about it than his mother, said comfortably, "She'll be a fool if she regards this as tantamount to a proposal, and an even greater fool if she puts the rumor about. He'll cut her off if she does, and I think she realizes that. As for what others might think, it's generally known she is in his keeping and would be expected to help with the preparations, since he hasn't a wife."

"But he has me!" Her grace, stung, protested. "Or Maria! Or even Joanna! And there is a difference, Miles, between having her preside over a dinner party where the only women present are ladies of the demi-monde, and have her oversee the preparations for a large ball! You may be sure that others will distinguish the difference, even if you can't!"

"But he hasn't asked her to act as his hostess, Mama," Miles pointed out reasonably. "And he doesn't intend to marry her, either. *I* know. She's been bombarding him with notes and messages for weeks and he's been neglecting her. Personally, I would not be surprised if he drops her after this."

Her grace wanted to believe it, but she had

very little faith in Miles's judgment, and the overwhelming evidence was to the contrary. And a day or two later, when the next snippet reached her by way of Céleste, her grace saw it as conclusive. In great agitation, she sent for Joanna so that Céleste could relate it to her, then interrupted and told it herself.

"Simon's servants are threatening to resign, and it the eve of the ball, and all because of that woman! She has brought in a pastry-cook, thereby offending Alphonse, whom Simon lured away from the Duke of Argyll by promising him the earth—not that I hold with having a tyrant in the kitchen—but the point is, Simon would be *furious* if you or I did such a thing! Alphonse has threatened to leave, not to mention Shellton and Mrs. Twicklesham, who have been with Simon since his father's time, and are almost as much a fixture as Nanny, who cared for him as a baby—Arkwright, I mean, not Simon, although she cared for Simon, too, by coming to Somerlea and simply refusing to budge! Charles said to let her stay . . ." With an effort, her grace abandoned the side issue of Nanny and Simon's babyhood, not to mention Charles's injunctions, and returned to the main point. "Shellton and Mrs. Twicklesham have been mortally offended. Mrs. T. says she does not intend to take orders from a harlot, and if she is brought in as 'my lady,' she will go. And Shellton is insulted that Lady Lindsay is attending to the bills personally, for he always does the household books. Of course, it gives her endless excuses to consult

with Simon! And—and one of the footmen overheard her informing the caterer that she was
soon to be wed to his lordship!" This, obviously,
was the shattering point to her story and she
finished with a flourish of her handkerchief.
"It makes me ill to think of it!" she wailed.

Joanna, to whom this news had struck as
sharply as a dagger to the heart, did not pause
to question why but replied in a colorless voice,
"Ma'am, I know you're unhappy about it, b-but
if he loves Lady Lindsay..."

"Love!" Her grace's voice was filled with
loathing. "Lust, you mean! He is a fool!"

Joanna said nothing. She was too shaken to
discuss it. Her reaction to the news of his im-
pending marriage had made her know the
truth: without realizing it, she had fallen in
love with Lord Arkwright, a man who regarded
her as a harlot as well as a liar. Her case was
hopeless—the best she could hope for was to
guard her secret from him, for he would be
amused by her presumption. As for Lady Lindsay, like Shellton and Mrs. Twicklesham, she
would have preferred to see him love someone
more worthy.

Shellton would never have dreamed of mentioning it to his master, naturally, for he knew
him well enough to know he would never allow
any of his servants to question any decision he
ever made, certainly not his choice of a wife.
But he was wise enough to know that he might
put a spoke in the lady's wheel through the
duke, so he went to his grace. Miles, shaken to

hear that a domestic crisis of major proportions was brewing on the very morning of the ball, hunted Simon down until he found him at his desk, looking over the bills that had arrived. Dutifully, Miles repeated what he had been told and ended with Shellton's threat of a servant walkout. Simon was inclined to take the matter lightly.

"It doesn't sound to me that any of the servants have anything to complain of," he said mildly. "Lady Lindsay merely has been doing as she was requested—by me."

"Shellton says she has been insulting."

"My dear Miles," his cousin murmured. "If you must listen to servants' gossip, then you deserve to be alarmed by their threats. So far as Shellton and Mrs. Twicklesham are concerned, they would no more leave my service than I would discharge them, and they know it." His lordship's eyes twinkled as he visualized the Banbury tale that old Shellton had been pitching his young and impressionable cousin.

"But Lady Lindsay questioned Shellton's integrity when she took over the party bills."

"Nonsense. If he told you that, it's because he wants you to fight his battles for him," Simon drawled. "He knows this party was to be supervised by her, and he is perfectly capable of flattening her with a few well-chosen words if she interferes in his domain."

"He wouldn't care to come to points with your future wife." Miles pointed out carefully.

Unlike Shellton, he did not believe Simon

would be so besotted as to wed a woman of Lady Lindsay's reputation, but he had been taken aback by her outright declaration to some of the workmen in the house. Therefore, he watched closely to judge Simon's reaction and was disappointed to see that he remained impassive, unless one counted a slight clenching of the hand that held a bill.

"Dear me," Simon murmured. "Where did you get that bit of information? Don't tell me that Lady Lindsay was so indiscreet as to announce our betrothal to Shellton?"

Miles did not quite like the choice of words. They denied nothing.

"No," he said defensively. "She did not. However, she was overheard announcing to the florist and the caterer that she was the future Lady Arkwright. I—I did not know if it was true or not," he added awkwardly.

Now Simon was angry. His face paled and sharpened but he said nothing at first. Then, through gritted teeth, "Stupid bitch! How like her to anticipate from nothing more than a mere request! Never mind. I shall have to make her position clear to her beyond a shadow of a doubt. I really must curb my desire to tease my aunt," he added plaintively, a statement that made absolutely no sense to Miles, but nevertheless reassured him enormously.

The night of the ball, Miles came at an early hour to escort his mother back to the Arkwright mansion. They were both to stand as hosts with Lord Arkwright to receive the guests. Joanna was told that her grace had already left when Céleste came to her room to assist her in dressing for the ball.

Joanna's costume had been found in a trunk in the attic. It had belonged to Lady Mary Catesby, who had married the 8th Duke of Somerton, and had lived just long enough for her portrait to be painted in the dress and hung in the gallery of Somerton House. The Lady Mary had been a Reformation duchess and a great beauty of her day, and her dress fitted Joanna as though it was made for her. It was fashioned of midnight blue velvet with a stand-up ruff encrusted with lace and gold thread. The bodice was revealing, and sewn with thousands of small pearls, with pearl drops dangling from the points of the long embroidered sleeves. Céleste's clever hands had copied Lady Mary's hairstyle so well that it could have been the lady herself standing before the mirror.

Joanna thought of this ball as her last fling. Whatever happened tonight, she knew she would be leaving tomorrow. Letitia Witherspoon had written her; a kind letter, inviting her to come to Watford, the little village where she was spending the summer. Money for her fare was enclosed. Joanna was unhappy to leave Georgie, but she no longer believed that Miles would banish him to Yorkshire to live alone. He—they all—were too kind. That threat had been one of Lord Arkwright's little punishments.

But she could not hate him, even now, and

if she could be granted one boon tonight, it would be to have the opportunity to dance with him at least once. After that, she promised herself fiercely, she would be happy to go to Watford.

She was to accompany Lord and Lady Houghton to the ball. By the time their carriage reached Green Street, it was choked with traffic and there was a long line crawling slowly toward the Arkwright mansion. Link-boys carrying flaring torches lined the street and lighted the entrance as the carriages pulled up, one by one, to discharge their passengers. The mansion doors had been flung open to disclose a glittering scene within and the unruly crowd, that was being held back by burly footmen, divided their attention between it and the arriving guests. There was a rumor afoot that the Prince Regent was expected, so the group was larger and more vocal than usual.

As they stepped from the carriage, Lord Houghton, who was dressed as a Roman senator, came in for some rough chaffing and a few ribald comments. His dignity was affronted by the time he reached the safety of indoors.

"My word," he puffed, "can't Arkwright do something about that group of ruffians collected at his door?"

"You are a member of the House," his wife reminded him. "Why don't you introduce a bill?"

Fortunately for Joanna's gravity, they were interrupted by a servant who took their cloaks and directed them to go forward.

They then joined the guests that were thronging up the great double staircase toward the ballroom on the upper floor. Joanna, who had never seen Lord Arkwright's home before, looked around with considerable awe. The staircase led from a magnificent entrance hall patterned in checkerboard squares of black and white marble. An enormous chandelier, suspended from the ceiling, glittered above the heads of the costumed guests below. Mingling with the guests were the servants, slipping through the throng with trays. Occasionally, above the noise and confusion inside, one could hear the sound of carriage wheels and the muted roar of the crowd greeting each new arrival.

At the top of the stairs, his lordship, accompanied by his aunt and his cousin, greeted their guests as they were announced by Shellton. The hosts reserved for themselves the privilege of not wearing costume. His lordship and the duke were in formal dress, and her grace wore a ball gown of frosty ice-blue, with diamonds at her throat and ears.

"You make a—delectable Elizabethan, Mrs. Martingale," Lord Arkwright murmured, bending over her hand. He seemed like a stranger, a very striking stranger, and for once there was no animosity. Joanna felt unaccountably shy. "Are you Mary of Scots?"

"No," she stammered. "I am Lady Mary."

"Oh, yes. The dark-haired beauty in the Long Gallery. You have certainly captured the—essence of the portrait. I have always been glad she was saved from the axe." His eyes lingered on Joanna's white throat and shoulders.

She moved on, slightly shaken by the look in his eyes. The Houghtons were ahead of her, and blindly she followed their broad backs as they led the way into the ballroom, which was a long room lined with mirrors. It had been decorated for the ball with profusely massed baskets of flowers, and their scent was so overpowering that the windows leading onto the balcony had been thrown open to allow air. Some of the chaperones were looking disapproving, aware that their charges might slip away and join the couples already melting into the shadows outside.

Lord Houghton made his way to the card room, leaving his lady to find her way over to where some of her friends sat, among the chaperones, against the wall. Joanna was following her reluctantly, looking longingly over her shoulder at the costumed dancers. A dance had just ended; another would soon begin, and suddenly a sadfaced Harlequin appeared at her elbow.

"How do you do, Mrs. Martingale? How do you do, Lady Houghton?"

"Why, Sir Humphrey, how well you look in costume." Maria smiled brightly at him. "I wondered when you would be returning from Derbyshire. It doesn't do to stay away too long. Surely you know that a faint heart never won a fair lady?" she added coyly. Joanna's teeth gnashed with frustration.

To her surprise, Sir Humphrey did not respond with his usual heavy gallantry. He looked haunted and inquired, "I wonder if you would give me the pleasure of this next dance, Mrs. Martingale?"

As they took their places in the set, Joanna was conscious of a stirring of curiosity. Sir Humphrey was disturbed about something: his attitude was more resigned than pompous.

"Your costume is very good," she said tentatively.

"Thank you, Mrs. Martingale. Ordinarily, I do not attend costume balls, but I made a special effort tonight because I wished to see you. Er—have you given any more consideration to that proposal I made to you the other day?"

They were separated by the dance, and when he returned she had her answer ready.

"It simply won't do, Sir Humphrey. I regret but—we are not suited."

Far from looking grieved or offended, Joanna thought she detected relief. His next words confirmed it. "Yes, I agree with you. It would not be wise. My mother is most distressed, most displeased by my choice. Even the news that you were related to the Houghtons..." He sighed. "When I left, she was ill. The doctor had prescribed rest and quiet. She has palpitations, you know, and mustn't be distressed. I am afraid I have given her a great deal of cause to be distressed this past week." He sighed again. "Yes, our marriage would have been a mistake."

"She would have lived with us, then?" Joanna

asked gently, mastering a hysterical desire to laugh.

"Oh, yes, yes, indeed. She refused to retire to the dower house, so it would have meant.... Oh, yes, indeed, she would have lived with me and my wife. As you can see, there would have been discord. My mother pointed out to me that a widow, one who has been used to ordering her own household, would not have done at all. A strong-minded woman such as yourself.... A man cannot live with discord in his own home, Mrs. Martingale."

She agreed fervently. "Your mother, no doubt, has chosen someone else whom she thinks would be more suitable, hasn't she, Sir Humphrey?" she asked sweetly.

He could not deny it. "A young lady in the neighborhood. A very worthy young lady, you understand, a great favorite of my mother's, but..." he stopped and allowed Joanna's vivid imagination a moment to picture the worthy young lady.

"If I had said that I would marry you, what would you have done, Sir Humphrey?" she asked curiously.

A spasm of alarm crossed his face, then apparently he was reassured by a quick look at Joanna. "Naturally, I would have honored my obligation," he said firmly. "My mother would have been displeased, but I am a man of honor. It would not have been a happy arrangement, but my mother would have made the best of the bargain."

No, it would not have been happy, Joanna thought. The dance came to an end and they parted with a feeling of mutual relief on both sides.

"Needing rescue again, young Jo?"

It was Barry, dressed as Robin Hood in doublet and hose. He was grinning.

"No. I think I have just been given my congé. It seems that Sir Humphrey's mother does not approve of me." She unfurled her fan. "Is it always this hot?"

"This is nothing. Wait until the Prince arrives. He doesn't like drafts, so the windows will be closed."

"Is he really coming?"

"Oh, I should think so," he replied easily. "He is a great friend of our hosts. Speaking of Lord Arkwright, have you noticed La Lindsay tonight? She is holding court across the room and flirting in an outrageous manner. The rumor is rife that she and Arkwright have quarreled and she is bringing him to heel."

Joanna looked in the direction he had indicated. Marjorie Lindsay was dressed in green silk, in the style of the French court a century earlier. She was easily the most beautiful woman on the floor. She was wearing a Madame Pompadour wig and a spray of diamonds glittered in the powdered tresses. In fact, Marjorie was sparkling with diamonds, gifts, no doubt, from her lovers. She was surrounded by several gentlemen and from the laughter coming from her circle, the incomparable Marjorie was apparently enjoying herself thoroughly. And attracting a great deal of unfavorable attention.

There was nothing in her countenance to indicate that she had just been dealt a stunning snub by his lordship when he greeted her with cold indifference. There had been nothing mentioned about her part in making this ball a success; no warm look in his eyes to indicate that he understood that hers had been the planning, the direction. Merely coolness before he turned to the next guest, leaving her dazedly trying to understand what had happened.

She had been accompanied by Bobby Uxham and Lord Naylor, two wealthy young men who were forever hanging about her and who, either of them, would have given a fortune to cut Lord Arkwright out at a word from her. Could he have been jealous of one of them? Surely not! As she passed into the ballroom, puzzled, burning with resentment, almost the first person she saw was—that woman—that Martingale woman.

She had known, then. There had been a glow about her that could only mean the chit was in love and not with that bore, Sir Humphrey Mayhew, with whom she was dancing. Could that stunning woman be the pale, insignificant creature with whom she had shared a carriage days ago? Oh, part of it was the costume, of course, but that was small comfort, for many a man had been captivated for life on the basis of one night's enchantment. And his—coolness, his preoccupation, Marjorie now chose to call it, meant that he had been thinking of Joanna

Martingale when he greeted her! Marjorie was shaken but still in fighting form. She must keep her head, waste no time with anger, but think! Frankly, the matter was too serious for anger. She must be clever. In vain, she tried to remember anything Arkwright had said that was detrimental to the widow, but there was precious little that she could recall. She had never been a woman who enjoyed listening to a man talk about another female in her presence, so she had discouraged it. Although of late, and now this seemed significant, he had not even mentioned her name. And how long had it been since he had made love to her? That alone should have shown her which way the wind was blowing, for at one time he would have been panting for her. Well, only guile could help her now. Guile and strategy.

A great believer in the strategy of jealousy, Marjorie turned to the two youngsters beside her and bestowed a ravishing smile impartially upon both. By the time Joanna noticed her, she had succeeded in gaining quite a following, although she had continued to keep her angry eyes fixed upon Joanna.

Marjorie would have been very gratified to know that the rumor she longed to have started by the servants had at last begun to circulate the ballroom. Where it originated, no one knew: perhaps on the wind, but Barry mentioned it to Joanna.

"He won't like the attention she is getting.

No man likes his wife to be noticed that way in public."

"His *wife?*"

"Yes. I heard they are secretly betrothed. Of course, it could be untrue, but I doubt it. It is said that she helped in the planning of tonight's ball, and being well-born, he may forget her reputation long enough to marry her. However, if it isn't true," Barry added reflectively, "she would do well to quash it now, before any hint of it reaches his lordship's ears. He would be very angry."

"I am sure it is true." A little of the glow begun by Simon's compliment disappeared. "And apparently she does not think he will disapprove of her behavior."

"No," Barry admitted.

The music had begun again, a waltz, and since he had asked her for this dance, they were preparing to begin when the musicians faltered to a stop. A murmur swelled, then hushed, and the dancers began to fall back, making room for an aisle down the center of the room. The Prince Regent had arrived.

He was not the glamorous prince of the fairy tales, but a stout, middle-aged man. Accompanied by his hosts, the duchess and Lord Arkwright, with the duke trailing behind with several gentlemen who were members of his party, the Royal Person slowly made the round of the ballroom, pausing occasionally to greet a special friend. Joanna noticed that he invariably stopped when he came to a beautiful woman,

174

but she was shocked speechless when he paused before her.

"Ah, young Northcote, I see. And who is this pretty young lady, Lieutenant?"

Joanna dropped into a deep curtsey and Barry bowed, apparently struck drumb, also. It was Lord Arkwright who answered easily.

"This is Mrs. Martingale, Your Highness."

"Ah, a relative of yours, I take it?" he asked Miles genially. "And where is your husband, Mrs. Martingale? I would like to meet him."

"Mrs. Martingale is a widow, Your Highness," Barry said manfully.

"Ah! You dog!" His eyes relished the rosy color of Joanna's cheeks. "Such a *pretty* child. Will you save me a waltz, m'dear? I am very partial to waltzes," he added, moving on, leaving Joanna pale with the enormity of having been asked to waltz with her sovereign.

But her lesser triumph was lost in the flutter of attention that Marjorie commanded. His Highness stopped short to speak to her, and then prepared to remain indefinitely. The duchess, her face rigid with distaste, was forced to listen while he paid Marjorie fulsome compliments on her appearance, her costume, her faithful reproduction of the character of Madame Pompadour. All was said in a loud, bluff voice that could be heard throughout the room. Finally, motioning to the musicians to resume, he performed the coup de grâce. Ignoring his hostess, although she was of higher rank than Lady Lindsay and should have been his first choice, he escorted Marjorie out onto the floor as his first partner. She could not avoid a flash of triumph as she passed before her grace's outraged nose. His lordship, however, was expressionless as he bowed to his aunt and offered her his arm. Together, they followed their royal guest and the lady of his choice. The two couples circled the room, waltzing, then gradually they were joined by the remaining dancers.

When the dance ended, the Prince remained standing in the middle of the floor, and obviously he intended to ignore convention and make Marjorie his partner again. She was flushed with success and flirting outrageously, apparently lost to the fact that by flouting convention she was most certainly disgusting her lover. Could she have been so blind as to think she could bring him to heel by making him jealous of his Prince? Barry asked Joanna.

His lordship bowed to his aunt and turned her over to Lord Sidney who claimed her for the next dance. Then, with the eyes of the room watching him, he walked directly over to Joanna and bowed slightly.

"Mrs. Martingale," he said gravely, "the Prince has called for another waltz. Will you do me the honor?"

Even if this dance had been booked, she could not have denied him. This, she knew, was what she had been waiting for, the high point of the evening, the reason for the dress and even her presence at the ball. Without saying a word, she floated into his arms and they swung into the lilting movement of the waltz.

Neither spoke at first, then finally, he said jerkily, "You waltz very well, Joanna." He did not seem to notice his use of her name. "But then, you have had a great deal of experience, haven't you?"

Experience! On the basis of one painful evening at the Barton home and her two waltzes at the Castlemaine ball? She wanted to giggle, but managed to say solemnly, "Indeed I have, my lord. I was forever at a party in India."

"So I've heard," he replied caustically. "I hope you won't allow the Prince's compliments to go to your head. He is in the habit of praising every woman he speaks to, and it means nothing, I assure you. It would be a mistake to take him seriously."

She stared fixedly at his waistcoat button. "You sadden me, my lord. I had hoped I was pretty, as he said," she murmured provocatively.

"You know that you are," he said stiffly. "I meant that you must not refine too much upon his words."

"Then I am pretty but the Prince is insincere?"

What devil was prompting her to tease him? His face darkened ominously. "Insincere, no! But not to be taken seriously. I had thought you were too clever to be taken in by idle flattery!" They were near the doors, and with a swift movement that took her by surprise he whisked

177

her out onto the balcony. "We need to talk, you and I. It is long overdue."

The light streaming through the open doors served to make the balcony well illuminated, leaving dark pockets of shadows near the arches of stone. Lord Arkwright moved purposefully toward one of those shadowed enclosures. There were other couples who had sought the privacy of the balcony, but none were nearby and had it not been for an occasional glimpse of a white shirtfront or a lady's fluttering skirts, Joanna would have thought they were alone. The music was muted and languorous with the dreamy cadence of the waltz. Joanna began to understand the anxiety of the chaperones who looked with disapproval at the open balcony doors.

"What is it?" She looked up. His lordship's face was a white blur above her.

"You seem to be extraordinarily vulnerable to flattery," he said harshly. "I suspect that that is how George Martingale had his way with you."

She stiffened. "George Martingale did not have his way with me!"

"Don't be absurd," he remarked dryly. "You may pass yourself off as a woman of experience but I think, in spite of your past, you have been led into this crime through nothing more than a suggestible nature. At any rate, you are apparently easily swayed by any plausible scoundrel who comes along. Perhaps, if you had been taken in hand at an early age before George got his hands on you, you could have been saved from your present folly. Whatever the reason, however, one cannot approve of theft."

"T-theft?"

He shrugged. "Call it what you will. Perhaps you pander to your conscience by pretending you have a right to what you have taken. But you and I both know that is sophistry. Theft is theft, whether you or an accomplice does it."

His words seemed extraordinarily severe if he was judging her on the basis of nothing more than her first ill-considered interview and Barry's words—words that he had later retracted. Yet, he felt himself justified in calling her a thief—a puzzling term, unless he had somehow learned that she was Joanna Marlbern, and was referring to the expensive wardrobe which the duchess had bought for her under false pretences.

His next words proved that he was. "I would have sworn you were genuinely fond of my aunt, yet you must surely know how you hurt her by what you are doing. The longer you deceive her and put off leaving—and don't tell me you haven't every intention of leaving—the harder it will be for her. She has grown fond of you. Don't you think of her in a compassionate way at all?"

"I—I—d-did n-not realize y-you would find t-the truth about me so—so unpalatable," she stammered haltingly.

He gripped her arms and shook her slightly. "Unpalatable?" he snapped. "That is a mild word for what *I* think of you, but we are speaking of my aunt. *She* is the one who must be protected. And it is precisely for that reason that I am giving you this warning! You are to leave as soon as possible, without saying one word about what you have done. Oh, she will be hurt when you leave without an explanation, I grant you, but that disappointment will be nothing to the disgust she will feel if you stay."

Joanna's eyes searched his face. "You think it is so disgusting, then?" she asked slowly. "I know what you said that first day, in the carriage, but I thought since then, I—you knew me well enough not to believe it of me."

"It is precisely because I know you so well that I think you are stupid, rather than venal," he ground out savagely. "I am appalled, however, that you should think any of us can forget for an instant who and what you are!"

Joanna, who had been referring to his assertion that she had been George's mistress now saw that she had erred. Why, he cared nothing about that! Why should he, when he was going to marry his mistress? Neither did the duchess, in spite of her sweet, winning ways. No, he had not been talking about *that*! The evil—the shame—had been her position as the Martingale nursemaid, and when his lordship spoke of hurt and disgust he was referring to the embarrassment her grace would feel if her friends learned that she had presented a servant to them as an equal. No matter that the duchess had already known and had not seemed too disturbed about it. The point was that Simon thought she would! He thought she was—disgusting. It took a blithe, free spirit like Barry's to forget her former position and see the real Joanna. It took a warmhearted soul like Letitia Witherspoon to welcome her in spite of it!

"I will go tomorrow," she said stoically, trying to pull free of his hands.

"I know you will go tomorrow!" he snapped. "Don't you think I have guessed your plans, you little idiot? That is not what I want you to do."

"What then, Lord Arkwright?" she asked wearily. "I have already promised to leave. What more do you want?"

"Your assurance that you will go tonight, as soon as you can."

"Oh." She drew a quick, hurt breath. "So that is the real reason you were so angry with me for accepting the Prince's compliments? Perhaps you are afraid that I will waltz with him, and later he will blame you? Or is it that you think my continued presence will offend your guests? Why then did you even ask me to your horrid old ball?" Her voice trembled with fury. "Why did you even give a ball? Despite your assurances to the contrary, the duchess has told me repeatedly that it was given for me! Was that before you knew the contemptuous character I was? And will you pretend ignorance, take the easy way out, when she and the Houghtons ask why I have left? How will you explain throwing me out of your house?"

He stared into her angry, working face, his own scarcely less white with fury. "You tormenting little wildcat," he muttered, half under his breath. "You know I don't want you to leave, but I am trying to keep you out of prison! Why can't you get that through your stupid, empty, little head?"

His grip tightened insistently and before either of them was aware of what was happening, she was in his arms and he was kissing her ruthlessly, repeatedly. After the first shock of surprise, Joanna began to struggle furiously, only to find herself unable to move. Finally, when she lay quiescent in his arms, her struggles abandoned, her lips soft and yielding beneath his urgent, demanding mouth, he put her reluctantly aside.

"Damn!" he swore softly, his voice breaking off on the edge of a smothered, half embarrassed laugh. "I didn't intend that! Not—not with you."

It was certainly a tactless remark to make under the circumstances, but his lordship had obviously been shaken out of his normal, cool self-possession and spoke unthinkingly. Joanna, who was wrestling with the horrifying suspicion that she had returned his kisses—and he knew it—took fire.

"No, I know you did not intend to kiss me, Lord Arkwright. But I tell you you are a hypocrite! You don't think a nursemaid is good enough to mingle with your guests or live in your aunt's house, yet you *kiss* her! Oh, I am aware that you were merely indulging in a preliminary step to a seduction, but *I* happen to have some scruples, too! And I don't intend to take Lady Lindsay's place as your next mistress!"

The music had come to an end by this time, and the dancers did not notice the pretty girl in the blue costume who pushed her way so determinedly through their midst. She did not see anyone she knew, fortunately, since her eyes were blinded by unshed tears of self-laothing. Outside the ballroom door, she bumped into one of the maids.

"Will you get my cloak and call me a carriage?" she gasped.

"Of course, madam."

The woman may have been surprised by the abrupt request, but her voice was as impassive as though she was in the habit of escorting tearful girls out of ballrooms all the time. She led the way downstairs, Joanna stumbling after her. The stairs and hallway were deserted, and no one noticed them as they crossed the floor. Joanna concentrated on the knot of drab brown hair beneath the housemaid's cap, and followed the dowdy uniformed figure as though it was a lifeline.

In the cloakroom, she looked despairingly about before glimpsing the rich velvet cloak trimmed in fur that the duchess had lent her for the evening. As the maid lifted it from the rack, her hands caressed the supple velvet and her lips twisted derisively.

"It looks as though I did you a good turn by dying and leaving you to take my place, Joanna," she commented.

The voice, the manner, had changed. In some subtle way, the bland housemaid had shed her polite, colorless facade as though it was a second skin. Joanna looked up, momentarily startled out of her apathy by the metamorphosis, and found herself staring into the cold, blue eyes of Caroline Martingale.

The pounding in her head, which had begun upstairs as a headache, grew louder and as intense as a thousand drumbeats, and Joanna slid effortlessly into a faint.

CHAPTER X

WHEN JOANNA REGAINED consciousness, she was lying on the floor and Caroline Martingale was chafing her wrists. She thought she had only been out of her senses a couple of minutes, for the tears she had cried earlier were still wet on her cheeks.

"Caroline." She was merely mildly curious. "What are you doing here? You are dead."

"Don't be absurd!" Caroline said crossly. "Of course I am not dead! Would I be here if I were? Get up on your feet at once, before someone comes in and finds you lying on the floor!"

That brought Joanna to her feet as nothing else could have done—that and Caro's words and the reassuringly irritable, familiar voice. A dead Caroline would not sound like a live Caroline, not, that is, unless she Joanna was dead, too. But she was not, because her head was hurting where she had struck it when she fell.

She swayed slightly and Caroline supported her hastily.

"Can you walk?" she asked anxiously. "We have to talk, you and I, but we can't do it here. It's too public. There is a library on this floor. It's the room beside the stairs. Go there and wait for me. We will be private there."

"I'm dizzy." Joanna's fingers strayed toward her head.

"That can't be helped!" Caroline snapped. "We can't be seen together. You'll have to go alone. I'll bring you some wine."

Joanna obeyed her unquestioningly, as though she was fifteen years old again, and back in India. The library was dark and Joanna left the door ajar so that she would have enough light to grope her way to one of the windows. She threw it open and leaned out to breathe the cold, reviving air. She could hear the muted strains of music coming from the ballroom above. Her head felt better, although it still ached. She no longer felt dizzy, now that she knew she hadn't seen a ghost. She was still confused, but she knew that whatever Caroline was doing here, posing as a maidservant in Lord Arkwright's home, she was not dead.

A tinkle of glass alerted her and she turned as Caroline slipped into the room, carrying a tray of glasses. Joanna closed the window and started forward.

"Don't light a candle!" Caroline said sharply. "I don't want anyone coming in and seeing us together. I'll leave this door ajar for light, and if we talk low, no one will hear us. I brought you some brandy. It will make you feel better," she added in a more normal tone as Joanna approached the table.

"Thank you." Joanna accepted the brandy and took a cautious sip. Caroline, on the other hand, poured herself a generous measure and tossed it off nonchalantly.

"His lordship keeps an excellent wine cellar," she murmured ironically.

"What have you done to your hair?"

Caroline looked surprised, then laughed. "It's a wig, my innocent. A disguise. Just as the maid's uniform, the gray powder, the flat shoes and the flat voice are disguises. They are very effective, aren't they? If I hadn't spoken in my natural voice, you wouldn't have known me at all, would you?"

Joanna shrugged, looking at the brandy glass. She said nothing.

"You were crying when you came out of that ballroom. What happened? Did one of those grand people hurt your feelings?" Caroline added sarcastically.

"It's not important. What are you doing here disguised as a servant? You were reported killed by bandits. You and Lieutenant Ordway. What happened?"

"I might ask you the same thing," Caroline commented mockingly. "What are you doing here, impersonating me? You've been using my name, Joanna Marlbern!"

"How did you know?" Joanna asked curiously, then shrugged. "It doesn't matter. Nothing matters. Yes, I have been impersonating you. I had no choice. I had Georgie to care for and no money. If you remember, you stole the passage money."

"I needed it!" Caroline snapped. "But you—how did you get here without money? Did you write Lord Arkwright to send you more?"

"No, of course not!" Joanna was stung. "Colonel Barton paid our passage. Naturally, he assumed that we would be welcomed. You had given none of us any inkling of the way the Martingales felt about your husband. Or how—how unwelcome we would be. And I soon found out what he—his lordship—thought about me. Like most people, he immediately assumed that I was—had been—George's mistress."

"Naturally," Caroline remarked carelessly. "But we know better, don't we, my dear? I would have never allowed a viper in my own house if I thought for one minute there was any danger of *that*! At any rate, you were obviously not turned away in spite of your cold reception."

"Georgie was a baby. No one turns a baby away from his door."

"Why then did you find it necessary to assume my identity? It seems to me that you would have fared better as yourself, Joanna Marlbern."

"There is no secret about it," Joanna said wearily. "I was met in Portsmouth by Lord Arkwright, and within a few minutes I learned how he felt about all of us. Particularly about Georgie. If the Duke of Somerton had learned that he was an orphan, Georgie would have been packed off to northern Scotland in the care of a tutor and I would have never seen him again."

"And for that, you pretended to be me?" Caroline asked curiously. "Not that I am condemning you, you understand! It was a sweet little move, setting you up for life, providing you with a meal ticket..."

"I didn't do it for that!" Joanna protested indignantly. "I did it for Georgie! Surely you, as his mother, can appreciate how I felt! To deliver him into the hands of a heartless stranger, within minutes of his arrival, and never see him again... Yes, I forced Lord Arkwright to allow me—us—to stay here, by blackmailing him..."

"How does one go about blackmailing Lord Arkwright? I should have thought it well nigh impossible."

"I threatened to make a scandal. He thought that I was going to sell myself." Joanna gulped, looking back over that first interview with its tangle of misunderstandings. "It is all so mixed up."

"It must be, if he thought *you* would sell yourself into prostitution. An innocent like you! But then, he thought you were George's mistress. Couldn't he tell you were nothing but a stupid little nursemaid? My God, what must he have thought of George, if he believed he would shackle himself to a baby like you," she added contemptuously.

"He doesn't think much of George, and even less of you."

Caroline drew in a sharp breath. She did not much care for the new Joanna. "Very well, I suppose you've done me no harm, then, if you have kept yourself virtuous," she said grudgingly. "Knowing what a mouse you are, I am sure you have. For the time being, therefore, you have my permission to continue as *me*."

"No. No longer, Caroline. I want to stop. I have done enough harm already. I want to tell the Duke of Somerton the truth and go away."

"No, I won't allow it. I want things to remain just as they are for the time being. *I* will decide when you may go. And if you don't do just as I say, I will have you arrested for impersonation and thrown into jail, Joanna Marlbern! No doubt Lord Arkwright will have other charges to add to mine," she threatened.

"And what about you? You are impersonating a servant, and for far less noble reasons, I'll wager, than mine. Why didn't you return to Calcutta after that bandit attack? And what about Lieutenant Ordway? Is he alive, too?" She stared at Caroline, her eyes slowly widening. "I believe it was all a hoax. You weren't attacked by bandits at all, were you? You bribed the houseboy to lie to Colonel Barton and pretend you were dead! Why? Why?"

"You *are* clever, Joanna. I wondered if you would put two and two together. Yes, Ordway is alive and we did bribe his boy, because we wanted to elope to Rome. Without Georgie or his wife complicating our lives."

"How despicable you both are!" Joanna gasped. "But—that doesn't explain now. The way you are dressed and ... It has something to do with the Saxon Collection, doesn't it? You found the Collection among George's things, and you are selling it back to the duke! Aren't you, Caroline?"

"What do you know about the Saxon Collection?" Caroline asked suspiciously.

"Only what the duchess told me. But I do know it doesn't belong to you. George stole it from Somerlea."

"If you know what is good for you, you'll not breathe a word about me, or the Saxon Collection, or anything else," Caroline said menacingly. "If I reappear now, publicly, and tell everyone who I am, it will create quite a scandal for the Martingales, won't it? That precious duchess of yours will be very embarrassed. If you care about her—any of them—you won't want that, will you?"

"No," agreed Joanna reluctantly.

"Then you must return to Somerton House, and remain like a mouse in your room for another day or two, then you may babble your story to anyone you please. Do you understand?"

"I am not going to do it," Joanna said firmly. "I intend to go right now, and tell Lord Arkwright the whole thing!"

"Oh, no, you won't!"

Both of them had forgotten to keep their voices lowered. The door, which had been left ajar by Caroline, had allowed for eavesdropping. Marjorie Lindsay flung it open and swept in, her skirts rustling.

"We'll have some light, if you please!" Her voice crackled with authority. "I don't like to conduct my discussions in the dark. Besides, I want to see the real Mrs. Martingale." The door slammed behind her as she came forward and touched the lighted taper she was carrying to the branch of candles on the table.

The room, springing suddenly to life, was revealed as a library, lined with glass-fronted cases holding books. There was also a fireplace with an enormous brass hood and some heraldic flags draped from the ceiling. It was an enormous room and most of it was lost in shadows, but Joanna caught a glimmer of oil paintings on some of the walls.

"Who are you?" Caroline demanded bluntly.

"It doesn't matter. *Your* name is important. The real Mrs. Martingale!" Obviously, she had heard everything. "Lud, even with that fright wig on, you look more like young Northcote's description than she does!"

"Northcote? N-not Barry? Is he here?"

"In the flesh," Marjorie said dryly.

"Then—if he recognizes me, I must leave at once. Why didn't he give you away?" Caroline asked Joanna.

"I think he's her ally. Who is she, anyway?" Marjorie and Caroline had already made the cool discovery that they talked a similar language.

"She is Joanna Marlbern, my child's nursemaid."

"The little slut! How dare she pass herself off as a lady, a kinswoman of the Duke of Somerton, and presume to meet her betters on an equal footing? Why, she's nothing more than backstairs trash! That settles it! You are to leave immediately, slut, or I tell everyone who you are! Arkwright would have you stripped and thrown into the street if he knew the truth about you, and as for that precious aunt of his, she would have palpitations if I told everyone she had been foisting a serving slut on the *ton!*"

"Now, wait a minute," Caroline said uneasily. "It isn't *that* bad. Joanna's family is really quite respectable. Her mother..."

"Shut up!" Marjorie hissed viciously. "You haven't any bargaining power. I am the one who decides what goes on here. I overheard enough to know you are supposed to be dead and up to no good with that Saxon Collection. I have no reason to interfere with your affairs so long as you keep your mouth shut and stay out of my way. But—this bit of servant trash is another matter. She has gotten into my way! She has turned my lover against me, and I intend to see that she gets out of here at once, without saying a word to him, or anyone else. I don't intend for her to go wailing to him, earning his gratitude..." She turned to Joanna. "Unless you get out of here tonight, I shall make your story public. I am threatening to do just what the Martingale woman said she'd do—embarrass the duchess. Do you want that?"

"No."

"Then leave, unless you want me to make a laughingstock out of her grace. Is that understood?"

Caroline said philosophically, "Better do as she says." She picked up the tray of glasses. Obviously, she had written Joanna off in her own calculations.

"But what about Georgie?"

Caroline looked bored. "He is the duke's responsibility. Not mine. I suggest you leave him behind and go. This woman won't hold her tongue long, and Lord Arkwright might turn vindictive when he learns how you tricked him."

"Indeed I won't!" Marjorie announced.

They were leaving her alone. Apparently, Marjorie was willing to leave the mechanics of getting away to her, in order to return to the ballroom. As the door closed behind them, Joanna buried her face in her hands, a dry sob shaking her slender body. She had never felt so alone in the whole of her short life.

Suddenly, a faint scuffling from the direction of the windows alerted her to the realization that she was not alone. She jerked around, trembling, and called hoarsely, "Who is there?"

"It is I, Miss Marlbern." The curtains billowed, and Lord Arkwright stepped out from behind them. He was as suave and as impecbly elegant as ever, but there were several distinct differences. He had discarded his coat, and had slightly loosened the ruffled throat of his shirt, and he was wearing a very business-like pistol in the waistband of his trousers. The other oddity was more subtle. There was an air of suppressed happiness about him, as though, slightly beneath the surface, he was bubbling with exultation. "Are you going to be a—er—mouse, and do just as you were told by Lady Lindsay?" he asked with a wide grin. "Or do you have the courage to stay with me and strong-arm your oppressors?"

She had never seen him grin before. "Stay?" she asked uncertainly.

"Yes. Share my curtain with me. But you must make up your mind at once," he warned, "for Miles will be bringing him here soon. Well, which is it to be?"

"I'll stay," she said promptly, and wondered at herself.

"Good. No, not that way. Starnes is behind that curtain. Here, get into the window seat and prepare for a wait. Although I don't think it will be much longer."

Joanna curled up in the window seat. For the first time, she realized that his lordship had heard everything that had been said. He knew all about her, now, and he had heard Marjorie's threat to expose her. Yet, he hadn't seemed worried. He hadn't told her to flee so that Marjorie's vicious tongue could be stopped. Presum-

ably, he had better ways of handling Marjorie
She sighed slightly.

"Are you cold?" the murmur was in her ear
tickling her curls. Suddenly, she was sur
rounded by the snuggling warmth of velvet
"Have my coat. I had to remove it so I could get
at the pistol easily."

Joanna had forgotten the pistol. Did that
mean that he—Simon—expected to have to use
it? Could he possibly be hurt? Before she could
ask him, however, the library door opened, and
she saw, through the slit in the curtains, Miles
enter, followed by Lieutenant Ordway.

CHAPTER XI

JOANNA DID NOT recognize him at first for he was wearing the costume of an Indian, one of the hill tribesmen. There was the bulky, flowing robe, sashed at the waist; the turban wound around his head; the boots and shield, with a wicked looking dagger thrust into his sash. But most confusing of all was the beard, black and bushy, which completely hid the dark, swarthy face.

"Why this room?" Ordway asked curiously. Joanna started upon hearing his voice, but her gasp of recognition was quickly suppressed by Simon's warning hand upon her shoulder.

"This is the room where my cousin has his safe," Miles explained. "But I won't make a move to get the money until you get rid of that dagger. As you can see, I am not armed."

Ordway shrugged. "Oh, very well." He pulled the dagger out of his sash and tossed it upon a nearby table. "It was only part of the costume. I am not a killer."

"No," Miles agreed pleasantly. "Merely a thief and a womanizer. The point is—are you an Indian?"

"No. No use continuing with that part of the disguise, either." Ordway pulled a handkerchief out of his sleeve and began wiping the brown stain from his face and hands. "Why do you say 'womanizer'?" he asked reflectively.

"Don't deny that you are using Mrs. Martingale for your purposes? That you and she are in partnership?"

"No, I don't deny it," Ordway replied. "But you speak as though she was my innocent victim. I assure you," he added dryly, "she is not. It was her plan, from conception to finish. She inherited the Collection from Martingale and planned to sell it back to you. When she received Arkwright's letter, she realized that he would be a hard nut to crack, so she thought it best to approach the both of you—ah—obliquely."

"Obliquely!" Miles snorted. "Is that what you call it—this cat and mouse game of yours! Disguises—and demanding that the Collection be ransomed tonight, of all nights, during a costume ball! And most of all, demanding twenty thousand pounds for what is my own property! As for Mrs. Martingale, my cousin suspected her from the start! But don't try to tell me that it was her plan, for I wouldn't believe you."

Ordway shrugged. "Suit yourself." But he was obviously puzzled and behind her, Joanna indignantly sensed Simon's amusement. "At any rate, she is wise to every suit. She has a

rain for this sort of thing. However, this conversation is getting us nowhere. What about
the exchange? Where is the money?"

"Where is the Collection?"

Ordway laughed shortly. "I am wearing it."

"Wearing it? You mean—under your costume?"

For answer, Ordway carefully lifted the turban off his head. Beneath it, still on his head,
was the crown, glinting dully in the candlelight.
Miles reached for it eagerly but Ordway stepped
back. "The money first."

"Very well," Miles said reluctantly. "You
stand over there and remove the Collection from
wherever you are hiding it, and I'll get the
money from the safe. Then we will change
places and while you are counting the money,
I'll look over the Collection."

There was a silence. Ordway was apparently
considering the proposal for flaws. Finally, he
nodded and Miles moved over to a Van Dyck
portrait that Joanna had noticed earlier on the
wall. He pushed and it swung back, like a
hinged door, revealing a wall safe behind it.

Ordway whistled in admiration. "V-e-e-ery
nice!"

"Get busy," Miles snapped, bending to the
dial.

Ordway reached inside the deep turban and
lifted out the cup which had been nestling there.
He was wearing the armlet and ring. The last
was the plate, which had been apparently at-

tached to his wooden shield by a plastering of clay.

"Ingenious," Miles remarked sarcastically.

By this time, he had opened the safe and removed a satchel from it which he was placing on the table. "You may come here and count the money now, while I look over the Collection. And keep your hands above the table."

"Not very trusting, are you?" Ordway drawled, but he moved over to the table.

"Good boy," Simon breathed into Joanna's ear. "He has positioned him so that his back is to the windows."

Joanna knew now what he intended to do but there was danger still. Ordway might yet have a weapon on his person, and Joanna knew him well enough to know he was capable of using it if cornered.

Slowly, carefully, Simon eased himself out of the window seat, his hand gripping the pistol. The other curtain billowed and Joanna saw that Starnes was doing the same, and that he, too, held a weapon. Ordway's eyes—his attention—was all for the money, however, and he was taken completely by surprise when Simon placed the muzzle of his pistol to the back of his neck.

"Don't move a muscle, my man, if you value your life. Is it all there, Miles?"

"All here, Simon!" Miles was jubilant. "And without a shot being fired or anyone hurt."

"We're not out of the woods yet," Simon warned. "Hold your pistol on him, Starnes, while I tie his hands. You may come out now, Joanna," he added over his shoulder.

Miles started violently. "We can't trust her, Simon," he said quickly. "Did you overhear what that scoundrel said? I didn't believe it until then."

"You mustn't believe everything that our friend Ordway says." Simon's mockery was reserved for himself, too. He jerked Ordway's hands behind his back.

"You know my name?" Ordway eyed Joanna apprehensively.

"Yes, indeed." Simon said briskly. "I know all about your supposed death and the deception you practiced on your commanding officer. And about the real Mrs. Martingale."

There was a dead silence.

"I think about that matter, you are as puzzled as my cousin," Simon added. "Perhaps I can relieve you of your puzzlement, Miles, if you will allow me to introduce you to Miss Joanna Marlbern, spinster, who was Master Georgie Martingale's nursemaid."

Miles stared at her blankly. Joanna looked back at him apologetically. "I am sorry for misleading you about—who I was, your grace."

"I can't believe it," Miles sputtered.

"I think you must. Our little Miss Marlbern led us down the garden path, all the way." There was an air of suppressed delight about the way he said it that had Miles glancing at him in puzzlement. "The impersonation, however, was the result of my own impatient temper. We have been chasing shadows, you and I, Miles. Between us, we almost made it possible for George's widow to shift the blame for all this on Joanna's shoulders. As Ordway said, she has a brain for this sort of roguery. She saw the possibilities at once. And tomorrow, when they had gotten away—and I am sure they had some foolproof plan of escape—we would have been left with an innocent girl on our hands, who would have had no explanation for this theft and treachery."

Just then, a discreet knock sounded at the library door and Miles looked questioningly at Simon, his eyebrows raised.

"I think this will clear things up for you. Don't let him move, Starnes."

He stepped to the door and flung it open. A uniformed maid stood there. She looked slightly taken aback to be confronted by the master of the house. Her eyes darted past, located Miles, then Ordway, sitting on the sofa with a gun at his head. He was watching her resignedly.

Simon widened the door. "Come on in, Mrs. Martingale," he said ironically. "For once, we were a step ahead of you. The game is up."

Caroline came in reluctantly, her eyes darting blue fire at Arkwright.

"Miles, may I present the real Mrs. Martingale?"

"*She* is George's widow?"

"She is indeed. I think she deserves to be present while we discuss what is to be done with the pair of them. I am not disposed to be too easy upon her, considering that she was willing to use Joanna as her scapegoat—a girl whom she had taken into her home as a child, and used shamefully. It may not suit your notion of niceties to make a thorough search of the lady, Miles, but I think we may depend upon Starnes. She may be concealing a pistol and she is quite capable of producing it and blowing a hole through us. Ah! I thought so." Simon pocketed the dainty derringer Starnes produced from Caroline's sleeve. "Make that knot tight, will you, Starnes?"

The two captives sat side by side, sullenly, on the sofa. Simon considered them thoughtfully. Caroline's eyes shifted to Joanna, standing beside Simon, then back, apparently abandoning the thought of any help there.

"I hope you'll know me next time, my lord," she said in sarcastic mockery of his intense scrutiny. Even with the wig and ugly uniform, she exuded a bold sexuality.

"I was thinking of what Lady Lindsay said," he murmured. "Even now, dressed as you are, you are more what I expected from Lieutenant Northcote's description than Joanna ever was. I am amazed that I did not realize at once that she could never be you—not in a thousand years—particularly, after the boy's about-face. Oh, I was off my stride, floundering, I admit, but even so . . ." he stopped, as though suddenly aware that his two captives had no idea what he was talking about.

"The question is what to do with you," he

added briskly. "Much as I would enjoy clapping you two plausible scoundrels in prison, I don't think we can afford to. There is the child to think of, not to mention the family name, and the scandal it would bring down on all our heads. I presume there is also a Mrs. Ordway somewhere who would be further hurt by the knowledge that her husband was a thief as well as a philanderer." The prisoners watched him hopefully. "No," he said contemplatively, "I think we're going to have to get you out of the country as quietly and quickly as possible, and then pay you something to keep you away. It is galling to have to help a pair of rogues like you, but the truth would hurt too many persons. The arrangements can be made through our bankers in Rome. Not a large sum, but enough to begin a new life elsewhere. After that, I think we can safely leave it to Mrs. Martingale's ingenuity to keep you going."

"Then you're releasing us?" Caroline asked.

"Much against my better judgment, I am," Simon replied. "I think you both have the good sense to do as I say. I will expect you back here tomorrow morning, at which time we will work out all details and see to it that you're safely on your way to Rome. Miles," he added, "I'll leave it to you and Miss Marlbern to put away the Collection and the money while Starnes and I see this pair out a side door."

As soon as they had gone, Joanna began, "Miles—er—your grace . . ."

He looked up smilingly. "Miles."

"I don't understand why you allowed George to keep the Collection. If you knew he had it, why didn't you have the authorities in India search him and..."

"Family pride," Miles said briefly. "George counted on that, of course."

"But why did he steal it? It was a mad thing to do, and your mother told me it was not very valuable."

"It isn't," Miles agreed dryly. "To anyone but me. George stole the Collection for the same reason he kept it, the same reason I wanted it; it represents the authority of the family. Traditionally, the head of the family holds the Collection in his possession, and in George's mind it strengthened his claim that he was the rightful heir to the dukedom of Somerton. Of course, he hadn't a hope, for my father acknowledged me before my birth, but George hoped to muddy up the waters somehow, enough to make the claim stick."

"I don't understand why I never saw it in all those years. I didn't, you know," she added, wondering even now if he believed she was blameless.

"Seeing the clever way Ordway disguised the pieces on his person, I suspect he got the idea from George," Miles said matter of factly. "He probably had them secreted among his gear— there are dozens of ways—and even his wife mightn't have known where they were."

"Will this make any difference? About Georgie, I mean?" She asked tentatively.

"Of course not!" he said indignantly. "I would never punish an innocent child, particularly now that I have seen how little his real mother cares for him. You are not going?" he added quickly.

"I think I must. Thank you—for everything."

"Simon won't like it," he said uneasily.

"He won't care," she said brightly. "He expects me to go, tonight. I'll find Lady Houghton and ask her to send me home."

Miles frowned slightly. "Are you sure? I thought . . ."

"I am sure of one thing, your grace. I must go. Now," she added desperately.

She would have looked for Maria, but she saw Barry Northcote first and when she asked him to take her home, after one look at her white face he did so without questioning her.

CHAPTER XII

JOANNA HAD NO trouble reaching Watford, for Letitia's instructions had been carefully explicit, even as to which posting inn she must depart from.

Returning to Somerton House that night with Barry, she had pleaded a headache and sent him back to the ball. It had not taken her long to pack a portmanteau with only those items that she thought she could use in her new life, which excluded most of the pretty new dresses the duchess had bought for her. She had been surprised at how easily she was able to leave. For once, the vast hallway was empty of servants, and no one saw her creep out nor noticed her going toward the hack-stand around the corner, where she found a cab to take her to the posting inn, a well known one in the north of London. There, she melted in the crowd, and at dawn, concealing her modish gown of French cambric beneath her old gray cloak, she clambered aboard the coach, clinging to her reticule in which reposed the last few shillings she had in the world.

No one had even noticed her then. Squeezed between a sleeping farmer and a stout lady who sucked peppermints and napped, she had not attracted the attention of anyone but a solemn-eyed baby sitting in his mother's lap. He had continued to watch her with an unnerving stare until finally, lulled by the motion of the coach, he had fallen asleep before the coach reached Watford and did not awaken when she made her departure from it there.

Letitia Witherspoon proved to be a younger, prettier version of her sister, but with the same flair for organization. She was increasing with the fifth little Witherspoon twig, and was encouraged by her spouse to spend her summer days in idleness. She was, therefore, ripe to take over the planning of Joanna's life. She had already decided that the best thing open to her was to become a governess, and with the help of Miss Makepeace, her children's governess, she had set out a course of studies for Joanna to follow. The idea was for her to become proficient enough to declare herself competent to teach. Miss Makepeace was to drill her in geography, writing and arithmetic, and Letitia, who was an expert needlewoman, would undertake that part of her instruction herself. After taking a look at Joanna's attempts to draw, it was generally agreed that she had better forego making any claim in art, and the less said about her music, too, the better.

It was vacation time for the older children, which made it an admirable time for the long suffering Miss Makepeace to take on Joanna's course of studies during her own precious hours of freedom. She uncomplainingly worked hard to repair the deficiencies of years of neglect, but it was uphill all the way, and Joanna was miserably conscious that she had no talent for teaching. The children, who seemed to regard her as a fellow sufferer, helped when they could, but nothing could make the return of her schooldays anything but a chore.

Joanna was thankful for Letitia's help, of course, and knew her interest was kindly meant. It was just that she had a stubborn habit of remembering the people at Somerton House, and try as she would, she could not prevent a lean, sardonic face from intruding itself upon the pages of her geography book. Sometimes she wondered if she had become that silliest of all creatures, a lovesick maiden yearning for the unattainable.

Mr. Witherspoon was a wealthy merchant in the City, and he suggested that he have his lawyer discreetly enquire into the matter and see if the Duke of Somerton would be agreeable to allowing Joanna to see Georgie occasionally. "Although," he added, "I must warn you that if he is not agreeable, you can do nothing about it. He is the boy's guardian, and you have no rights whatsoever. However, I see no reason why he shouldn't be cooperative after a—er—suitable interval of time has elapsed."

He was referring of course to her masquerade as Georgie's mama, of which he highly disapproved. In fact, so shocked had he been when he heard of it that his wife had thought better of mentioning the rest of the astounding story Joanna had told her. She soothed her conscience by reminding herself that he was a busy man, who spent most of his summer in the City adding to his already not inconsiderable fortune, and therefore, properly needed relaxation when he visited them in the country.

Joanna was outside in the garden, minding the two younger children, the afternoon that noble visitors arrived at the Witherspoon home. She was informed of guests by Nanny Dakers, the children's nurse, who hurried across the grass toward her. Nanny was jealous of her, for she was positive that Joanna's goal was to usurp her place, so whenever possible she managed to infer that Joanna was burning with resentment because she was excluded from Mrs. Witherspoon's social life.

There was a subtle sneer to her voice as she said, "The mistress has guests. I came out for these two, thinking you'd probably expect to join them in the parlor."

"Did Mrs. Witherspoon ask for me?" Joanna asked mildly, trying to ignore the old woman's rancor.

Nanny hesitated, then shrugged, so Joanna decided to take a walk. Nanny's taunts had made her sensitive to the realization that Letitia did, indeed, frequently include her whenever she had guests, and she was determined to avoid being thought pushy or forward.

She rose and shook out her muslin skirts. She was wearing the dress she had worn for dinner at Mockridge Hall and the memories it brought back touched her face with wistfulness for an instant, before she reminded herself sternly that she was fortunate to have such friends as the Witherspoons. It was not that she was ungrateful or did not recognize the importance of keeping one's nose to the grindstone; it was merely that when she foresaw the pattern of the future, she found it rather frightening.

To reach the front gate, it was necessary to pass the parlor windows and Joanna kept her face averted, hoping Letitia would not see her. There was an old-fashioned traveling carriage at the gate, splashed with mud and bearing a crest on its paneled door. Joanna was surprised, for the Witherspoons did not have friends among the aristocracy. From the handsome appearance of the horses, the visitor was not pinched for money. A stout, elderly coachman, still wrapped in winter woolies despite the soft weather, was perched upon the seat, and he stared at Joanna so intently that she almost spoke to him.

Her favorite walk was toward Watford. The lane was used mostly by persons on foot and farmcarts, and this time of day was sure to be deserted. As she walked, Joanna was dismayed by the swift passage of the seasons. The cold day of her arrival in England seemed part of a dream now. It had been April and she had been looking forward to an English spring, but in London, spring had manifested itself in the flowers being sold on the street corners. She had missed her spring and now, she thought wistfully, summer was slipping by all too rapidly.

She had not gone far when she realized that someone was following her, running to catch up to her. She turned, half expecting to see one of the children, and to her astonishment, saw that it was Lord Arkwright. He came pounding up and stopped, panting. He did not look his usual smooth, unruffled self; he looked hot and angry, and his first words were irritable.

"What a tiresome female you are, Miss Marlbern! Do you always make a practice of running away when you get a message that you have guests!"

"I . . ."

"I shouldn't have been surprised. You never do the expected thing! You are the most perverse woman I have ever known."

"And you are the most arrogant and dictatorial man I have ever known!" Joanna snapped angrily.

He smiled, a singularly arch and sunny smile that broke his face into laughter. Joanna reflected bitterly that it was just like him to use his charm to win his point. Her heart was behaving strangely, no doubt as a result of this unexpected meeting, but she had no intention of allowing him to win their quarrel. She opened her mouth, then closed it abruptly, as she saw him watching her expectantly.

Swallowing her words with difficulty, she asked sweetly, "Why are you here, my lord?"

"Now what can I say that will carry the greatest weight with you?" he asked as if to himself. He cast a sidelong glance at her. "Perhaps if I told you that Georgie wanted you badly, in spite of his new pony and his dog, and I was here to bring you back, that would do it?" When she said nothing, he added mockingly, "Obviously, it won't. Very well, then, let us say that I am here to bring your Scottish grandfather to meet you."

"My *grandfather?*"

"Yes. Peter David MacAllan, the Laird of Glenachan. He wrote me when he learned from the landlord of the inn at Twickford-on-the-Sea that I had been making enquiries about you. His letter arrived the morning after the ball. I had just learned that you were missing, and I fear was not in the mood to appreciate the difficulties that his very unwelcome letter would put me to. On the one hand, I had a great deal to do in running you to earth. On the other, there was my aunt, who was having hysterics and blaming Miles and myself for your disappearance. She informed us that she had known all along your true identity, but had not informed us because of our prejudice. Altogether a most—er—illuminating conversation."

"You said—my grandfather's letter was unwelcome?"

"Yes, indeed. It did not appeal to me just then to have him turn up, breathing fire and demanding to take you back to Scotland with him. However, late events proved that a grandfather who was also a noble Scottish laird would be a convenience. That is when I left for Scotland, to bring him back with me. Otherwise, I would have been in Watford the day after you arrived." By this time, he had tucked her hand under his arm and was leading her back toward the Witherspoon cottage. "Of course, we learned almost at once where you were—from Georgie." He grinned. "That brilliant inspiration—to question the boy—came from Miles. He knew that you would never have left without reassuring him in some way, so we had the lad downstairs and asked him about it. He told us all about the talisman you left with him—the envelope addressed to you here in Watford. He told us that you had awakened him that night and told him if he was ever lonely or frightened, or needed him, he was to put it on the table with the other post, and you would come to him. Miles and I thought him an exceptionally bright boy to remember all of that."

They were within sight of the cottage now and his lordship, glancing at the coachman, remarked casually, "Timothy tells me that you look remarkably like your mother."

"My lord, is—does Georgie need me?"

He hesitated, then said, "No. He has decided to make his cousin Miles his hero now. They are at Somerlea right now."

An ill-assorted group was awaiting them in the parlor. Letitia Witherspoon, with a faint air of disapproval, was pouring tea for the guests, the Duchess of Somerton and Laird MacAllan. Joanna perceived at once a chill in the atmosphere, a coolness that indicated that there had recently been a frosty passage between some, or all, of the persons present. The duchess was dressed in one of her extremes of fashion, a semi-transparent gown of lavender jaconet muslin with a deep flounce and yellow kid boots. An upstanding poke bonnet, tied under her chin with long yellow ribbons, framed her pretty face. She was propping one hand, gloved in a lace mitt, upon the long handle of a yellow parasol that had been furled and tied with multicolored streamers. If she had tried, she could not have dressed in a fashion more likely to have gained the disapproval of a middle class, Methodist wife of a City merchant. Letitia, stodgy, pregnant, and very much on her dignity in her starched tucker and muslin cap, obviously thought her wicked and decadent.

Opposite them both, in a chair, was a grim-looking old gentleman with a mane of white hair. He was dressed in good taste, but like his carriage, there was an old-fashioned look about his appearance. As he stood up erectly to greet her, Joanna saw that he had her mother's eyes.

"Sir, may I present to you your granddaughter, Miss Marlbern. Joanna, this is your grandfather who has come to take you back to Scotland with him." Her grandfather embraced her stiffly. His lordship, having set the cat among the pigeons, retired from the fray and watched the battle develop.

The first to recover was the duchess. "Nonsense, Simon." She lifted a powdery cheek to be kissed by Joanna. "The child will naturally wish to visit her grandparents, and I applaud such a worthy sentiment, but her home is with me. I am in the process of bringing her into Society and I have a natural first claim on her time."

Joanna sat down beside her upon the sofa and smiled rather nervously and appeasingly at the other two.

"You, madam, have no claim at all," her grandfather growled. "As I have been telling you all the way to this place, her home is with me and her grandmother, not you."

"And what will you do for her?" the duchess asked sweetly. "You told me this is your first visit to London in ten years! Do you plan to take her back to Scotland, and keep her secluded for the rest of her life among hills and glens! What opportunity would she have, in that case?"

"The same opportunity her mother had!"

"And look where it got her! You turned her out the first time she crossed your will!"

The old man's face reddened ominously. "I see that I was wrong to think I could rely upon your discretion, madam!" he roared. "Women can seldom hold their tongues when they are told a secret!"

"Oh, please..." Joanna began.

Letitia interrupted her. She had been listening with growing irritation. She disliked the duchess very much, but so far as she could see this autocratic old man was not much better. "You both would be well-advised to allow Joanna to decide for herself what she wants to do with her future," she snapped. "She is a liberated young woman. She does not want the frivolous life of a social butterfly, destined to marry a foppish nobleman who spends all of his waking hours trying to decide how to tie his cravat! Neither does she need what you are offering her, my lord—banishment to Scotland merely to become a comfort for you in your old age! She wants a career!"

The duchess, who found the latter part of this statement acceptable, took umbrage with the first part. "Social butterfly, indeed!" she remarked icily. "You, my good woman, are hardly in a position to criticize a Society with which you are obviously unacquainted! At least, with me, Joanna will have an opportunity to become someone's wife. That should be preferable to an existence as a poorly paid governess!"

Joanna burst into overwrought tears. She was crying too hard to hear the incoherent murmurs of sympathy from her grandfather, or the acrimonious passage between Letitia and her grace as they blamed each other, before the door shut upon them. The first thing she knew, a handkerchief was thrust into her hands and a voice, deepening with undertones of laughter, drawled, "Mop up, little one. They're all gone. Your tears did the trick."

Joanna mopped her eyes and sniffed resentfully, "Why didn't you join them? Or did you want to see if I could provide you with more amusement?"

"Oh, no, you don't draw me into a slanging match with you, my girl. I have become accustomed to your methods by now. I didn't join them," he added briskly, seating himself beside her, "because I told them if they would leave us alone together, I thought we would solve their problem for them."

"Oh?" She eyed him balefully over the folds of the snowy handkerchief. "How do you propose to do that? There is no way I can stay with one without hurting the other two! And I don't want to do that. E-even Letitia—Mrs. Witherspoon . . ."

"Oh? So you don't want to become a liberated woman, after all?"

Joanna sniffed again. "It might be the best thing to do," she muttered. "I cannot return to London, and I am not sure I want to live in Scotland."

"Your grandfather would never allow you to become a governess."

"I could do it under an assumed name."

"Now you're being provocative," he retorted mildly. "No, I think it is a much better solution for you to marry me. None of them can then claim that the other has received preference. Don't you think so?"

"Y-you're being absurd!" Her face was flushed

and her eyes flashed blue darts. "You don't love me. Why should you marry me to provide a solution to *my* problem? It is not as though I was an heiress—or—or was beautiful, or even of high rank. Moreover, if you married me, Lady Lindsay would make a scandal about me."

"No, she won't!" he replied promptly. "She has enough sense not to make such a fool of herself. When I suggested that she see about making other arrangements for her future maintenance, she . . ." Suddenly, he stopped and laughed wryly. "I should not be discussing a subject like this with you, but unfortunately I have gotten into the habit of saying anything I like to you, and I find myself unable to curb my tongue when I am in your presence."

"No, my lord," Joanna agreed primly. Her heart sang; she found his rough, half embarrassed words immensely satisfying. "You were saying about Lady Lindsay?"

He grinned slightly. "I was saying that I told the lady that she must call upon one of her many admirers to provide for her in the future, as I was no longer interested. She became rather abusive, threatening to make you the talk of the *ton*. By that time, I had received your grandfather's letter, and for the first time, appreciated it. I informed her that she was speaking of the granddaughter of the Laird of Glenachan as well as the lady whom I hoped to make my wife. I also reminded her that in her vulnerable position, she could not afford to gain a reputation for gossip. A gentleman might be chary of taking a mistress who could not hold her tongue about his secrets."

Joanna gaped at him. The half dozen freckles that persisted, in spite of repeated applications of buttermilk paste, stood out in pale relief across the bridge of her small, uptilted nose. "You told her that you—hoped to marry me?" she whispered.

"I did. Moreover, my darling, whatever gave you the idea that I was hanging out for a rich wife or one of great rank? So far as your third objection is concerned, it is obvious that my opinion of your beauty differs materially from yours. And now," he added, drawing her firmly into his arms and lifting her chin with a warm palm, "if you will allow me, I will deal with the fourth." He covered her face with kisses, ending with her mouth that trembled beneath his possessive lips.

"H-how can you love me?" she stammered. "W-we always fight."

"I enjoy fighting with people I love," he said positively. "It is a bore to fight with my enemies. And whatever else I felt about you during our tumultous relationship, my dearest, I assure you, I never found you a bore. And now," he added, "what about you? Are you going to admit you love me? Will you marry me?"

She buried her flushed face in his shoulder. "You know I do," she murmured, "but—are you *quite* sure you want to?"

His lordship was proving the strength of his

conviction in a most satisfactory manner when the door opened and the duchess walked in.

"Simon, I have just had the most delightful inspiration about Barry Northcote," she trilled. "Now that Joanna can face the world under her own colors, what is to prevent us from inviting Lord and Lady Lindville to..." she stopped abruptly, her surprise clearly written on her face.

"Aunt Celia, if you mean what I think you mean, you can forget it!" Simon asserted frankly. "That young man gave me too many jealous moments for me to consider bringing him into the picture, now that I have partially bludgeoned Joanna into agreeing to marry me. No, Aunt, I think you had better resign yourself to making a trip to Scotland after all, where Joanna's grandfather will naturally expect to give her away in marriage."

"Scotland?"

"Yes. Scotland." Simon's eyes twinkled. "I assure you, Aunt, in spite of your apprehensions, you will find it pleasantly civilized. Meantime, you may close the door behind you."

The door slammed and Simon turned back to her, keeping his face grave with difficulty.

"Now that we have succeeded in quieting our most formidable adversary, do you think, sweetheart, that you could give me your answer before the horde descends? I am strongly tempted," he added, his eyes twinkling, "to lock the door and keep them all out."

221

"We-e-ell," Joanna drawled, mischievously, "Mrs. Witherspoon left the tea tray in here, so we won't starve. Wait! No, Simon, I didn't mean . . . !"